BLOC

Focusing on novels with contemporary concerns, Bantam New Fiction introduces some of the most exciting voices at work today. Look for these titles wherever Bantam New Fiction is sold:

WHITE PALACE by Glenn Savan
SOMEWHERE OFF THE COAST OF MAINE by Ann Hood
COYOTE by Lynn Vannucci
VARIATIONS IN THE NIGHT by Emily Listfield
LIFE DURING WARTIME by Lucius Shepard
THE HALLOWEEN BALL by James Howard Kunstler
PARACHUTE by Richard Lees
THUNDER ISLAND by James Howard Kunstler
WAITING TO VANISH by Ann Hood

BANTAM NEW FICTION

BLOCKBUSTER

PATRICIA MARX AND DOUGLAS G. MCGRATH

BANTAM BOOKS

TORONTO · NEW YORK · LONDON · SYDNEY · AUCKLAND

To Jean Doumanian

NOTE

Blockbuster is a work of fiction that tells the life story of the imaginary X.Y. Schwerdloff. Names, characters, places, and incidents depicted in Blockbuster are fictitious or are used fictitiously. The events and speeches in this novel are not real, nor are they intended to be so interpreted. For example, the speeches, essays, and article excerpts contained in Blockbuster are completely the product of the authors' imaginations and there is no intention to imply that any of the speakers or writers have actually delivered, written, or published these fictional pieces.

BLOCKBUSTER

A Bantam Book / August 1988

Library of Congress Cataloging-in-Publication Data

Marx, Patricia.
Blockbuster.

(Bantam new fiction)
I. McGrath, Douglas.   II. Title.
PS3563.A756B5   1988   813'.54   87-35072
ISBN 0-553-34498-6

Published simultaneously in the United States and Canada

Bantam Books are published by Bantam Books, a division of Bantam Doubleday Dell Publishing Group, Inc. Its trademark, consisting of the words "Bantam Books" and the portrayal of a rooster, is Registered in U.S. Patent and Trademark Office and in other countries. Marca Registrada. Bantam Books, 666 Fifth Avenue, New York, New York 10103.

PRINTED IN THE UNITED STATES OF AMERICA

FG   0 9 8 7 6 5 4 3 2 1

A WORD FROM THE AUTHORS

ONE CRISP SEPTEMBER DAY, WHEN AUTUMN FELL LIKE A FRUIT, WE RECEIVED A LETTER FROM JULIA SCHWERDLOFF BUSH, DAUGHTER OF THE MOVIE PIONEER X.Y. SCHWERDLOFF. "MY SISTER AMELIA AND I," THE LETTER BEGAN, "SO ENJOYED YOUR ARTICLE ABOUT THE MOTION PICTURE BUSINESS IN *THE WALL STREET JOURNAL* OF SEPTEMBER 5, 1983. IN ALL OUR YEARS OF READING ARTICLES ABOUT THE MOVIE BUSINESS, YOURS WAS THE BEST. SO IMPRESSED WERE AMELIA AND I, WE WOULD LIKE TO SPEAK TO YOU ABOUT WRITING A HISTORY OF FATHER'S STUDIO AND ITS RECENT TROUBLES YOU HAVE UNDOUBTEDLY READ ABOUT."

NATURALLY, WE WERE DELIGHTED TO RECEIVE THIS LETTER AND AGREED TO MEET THE SCHWERDLOFF SISTERS TO DISCUSS THEIR PROJECT. BEFORE OUR MEETING, WE MADE SURE TO LOOK UP THE ARTICLE. INDEED IT WAS A SUPERB PIECE OF REPORTING. WE WISHED WE HAD WRITTEN IT INSTEAD OF OUR ARTICLE IN THE SAME *WALL STREET JOURNAL* ABOUT HOW POLITICAL PRESSURE ON FARM TOOL EXPORTERS HAD CHANGED THE MANUFACTURE OF CORRUGATED CARDBOARD CARTONS.

WE MET THE SCHWERDLOFF SISTERS AS SOON AS POSSIBLE AND AGREED TO WRITE WHAT EVENTUALLY BECAME *BLOCKBUSTER*. WE WROTE THE BOOK AS AN ORAL HISTORY BECAUSE WE WANTED THE READER TO HEAR THE STORY AS WE HEARD IT, TOLD IN THE SAME VOICES.

DURING THE EARLY STAGES OF INTERVIEWING, WE WERE DIS-

1

MAYED TO SEE THAT OUR TAPE RECORDER INTIMIDATED MANY PEO-
PLE. THEREFORE, WE DEVELOPED A TECHNIQUE FOR PUTTING PEOPLE
AT EASE. PATTY DECORATED THE TAPE RECORDER WITH COLORED
FELT AND CUT PRETTY PICTURES OUT OF MAGAZINES AND GLUED
THEM ALL AROUND THE RECORDER. LATER, DOUG AFFIXED A NICE
SEASHELL TO THE HANDLE.

WE WERE FINED TWENTY-FIVE DOLLARS BY A WATCHDOG GROUP,
THE ORAL HISTORY GUILD, EAST. THE GUILD CLAIMED THAT THE
FELT AND SEASHELL "MAY HAVE DECEIVED SOME OF THOSE QUES-
TIONED ABOUT THE NATURE OF THE INTERVIEW." AFTER WE PAID
THE TWENTY-FIVE DOLLARS, THOUGH, OLD MISS FUTTER CAME TO
US AS WE WERE PUTTING ON OUR COATS IN A LITTLE ROOM WITH A
FIREPLACE AND SOME PRETTY RED BOWLS AND TOLD US SHE REALLY
LIKED THE BOOK.

WE FELT AS PROUD THEN AS JAMES JOYCE PROBABLY DID WHEN
HE FINISHED HIS GREAT MASTERPIECE, *ULYSSES*.

CHAPTER 1

FADE IN: X.Y.
SCHWERDLOFF AND HIS STUDIO

WHEN RIVA SCHWERDLOFF GAVE BIRTH TO A SON ON NOVEMBER 28, 1895, SHE HAD LITTLE IDEA THAT HE WOULD SOMEDAY BE THE HEAD OF THE MOST PRESTIGIOUS MOVIE STUDIO IN HOLLYWOOD AND NO IDEA WHATSOEVER THAT IN 1956 HE WOULD WIN THE IRVING THALBERG MEMORIAL AWARD AT THE OSCARS. SHE ONLY KNEW THAT WHEN SHE PUT A PILLOW OVER HIS FACE, THE CRYING STOPPED A LITTLE AND SHE COULD GET SOME SLEEP. THE BABY UNDER THAT PILLOW WAS MOVIE MOGUL X.Y. SCHWERDLOFF.

RIVA AND JOSEPH SCHWERDLOFF, IMMIGRANTS FROM ROMANIA, RAISED THEIR SON TO BE PROUD AND NEVER TO TAKE FROM OTHERS THOSE THINGS THAT HE COULD GET HIMSELF. THEY DID NOT GIVE HIM A NAME, BELIEVING THAT IF HE GAVE HIMSELF THE NAME, HE WOULD APPRECIATE IT MORE. AT THE AGE OF FOUR, THE BABY SCHWERDLOFF CHOSE THE NAME A.B., THE ONLY LETTERS HE KNEW. LATER HE CHANGED HIS NAME TO X.Y., THINKING A.B. SOUNDED TOO JEWISH.

IN 1910, SCHWERDLOFF LEFT THE FAMILY RUG BUSINESS TO FORM A MOTION PICTURE PRODUCTION COMPANY WITH LOU PLOTZ, A FURRIER FROM THE BRONX, TO CAPITALIZE ON THE NATION'S BURGEONING INTEREST IN MOTION PICTURES. DURING THE EARLY YEARS OF THE MOVIE BUSINESS, AUDIENCES WERE SO FASCINATED BY THE

3

MERE IDEA OF MOVING PICTURES THAT THEY PAID LITTLE ATTENTION TO A FILM'S CONTENT. MOST OF THESE EARLY FILMS RAN NO LONGER THAN A FEW MINUTES AND CONSISTED OF A SINGLE INCIDENT.

THE FIRST PLOTZ-SCHWERDLOFF PRODUCTION, THE THREE-MINUTE *FOLDING THE WASH,* WHICH WAS ONE OF THE BIG MONEY-MAKERS OF 1910, IS CONSIDERED A MASTERPIECE OF ITS GENRE. FILM HISTORIANS CITE IT AS THE FIRST TIME SOMEONE SAT DOWN AND STOOD UP IN THE SAME MOVIE. PLOTZ AND SCHWERDLOFF FOLLOWED ITS SUCCESS WITH *OPENING THE CURTAINS, DIGGING A HOLE,* AND THE SIX-MINUTE *STRIPPING THE BED*—WHICH SO OFFENDED A GROUP OF CATHOLICS THEY FORMED THE CATHOLIC LEAGUE OF DECENCY.

A RIFT DEVELOPED BETWEEN PLOTZ AND SCHWERDLOFF WHEN SCHWERDLOFF WANTED TO INTRODUCE CHARACTERS AND STORIES INTO THEIR MOVIES AND PLOTZ OBJECTED. PLOTZ EVENTUALLY RESIGNED OVER THIS, FRUSTRATED THAT THE BUSINESS HE USED TO KNOW WAS GONE. "THE DAY I HEARD SOMEONE SAY, 'SUBPLOT,' " HE SAID, "I KNEW I WAS A STRANGER TO THIS BUSINESS."

AFTER PLOTZ'S RESIGNATION, SCHWERDLOFF RAN THE COMPANY SINGLE-HANDEDLY, SOON TRANSFORMING IT INTO A MAJOR STUDIO. THE FIRST THING SCHWERDLOFF DID WAS SELECT A LOGO. HE SELECTED HIMSELF. THE LOGO SHOWED SCHWERDLOFF IN HIS OFFICE, AT HIS DESK, ANSWERING THE PHONE. THIS IS THE ONLY KNOWN EXAMPLE OF A STUDIO USING ITS OWNER AS ITS SYMBOL OF EXCELLENCE.

AN ASTUTE PREDICTOR OF TRENDS IN THE INDUSTRY, SCHWERDLOFF MADE ONLY TWO MAJOR MISTAKES IN THOSE EARLY YEARS. THOUGH IT WAS HE WHO HAD THE IDEA OF SELLING FOOD IN THEATER LOBBIES, HIS IDEA—BAKED WINTER SQUASH—DID NOT CATCH ON. "I'LL NEVER UNDERSTAND THAT," SCHWERDLOFF SAID. "EVERY TIME WE HAVE IT AT THE HOUSE, PEOPLE ASK FOR SECONDS."

A MORE COSTLY MISTAKE WAS SCHWERDLOFF'S OPPOSITION TO TALKING PICTURES. HE FELT THE ADDITION OF SOUND WOULD LOSE THE INDUSTRY THE DEAF AUDIENCE AND POSSIBLY THE HARD OF HEARING AS WELL. "A LOT OF PEOPLE CAN HEAR A TALKING PICTURE," SCHWERDLOFF USED TO SAY, "BUT *EVERYONE* HEARS A SILENT

PICTURE." EVENTUALLY SCHWERDLOFF DID PRODUCE TALKING PICTURES, CONVINCED BY HIS PARENTS THAT THE DEAF WERE USING THE TITLE CARDS AS A CRUTCH AND COULD LEARN TO HEAR IF THEY REALLY NEEDED TO, IN THE SAME WAY THAT BABIES CAN LEARN TO SWIM IF YOU THROW THEM IN WATER.

THE MR. SCHWERDLOFF STUDIO PRODUCED FEWER MOVIES THAN THE OTHER MAJOR STUDIOS BUT SCHWERDLOFF KEPT TIGHT CONTROL OVER THEM. SOON THE STUDIO GAINED THE REPUTATION AS THE MOST PRESTIGIOUS IN HOLLYWOOD. IN ONE YEAR, THEIR FILMS *YOUNG CHARLEMAGNE, SURPRISE WITNESS,* AND *MISS VALOR IS HERE,* GARNERED TWENTY-FIVE ACADEMY AWARD NOMINATIONS.

AS THE HEAD OF THE MOST RESPECTED HOLLYWOOD STUDIO, SCHWERDLOFF WAS APPROACHED BY PRESIDENT ROOSEVELT AT THE OUTBREAK OF WORLD WAR II TO RALLY THE NATION AGAINST THE JAPANESE. IN 1943, THE STUDIO RELEASED *TOKYO, KANSAS,* A MOVIE ABOUT A JAPANESE LIBRARIAN IN A SMALL KANSAS TOWN WHO INSERTS PROPAGANDA INTO THE LIBRARY BOOKS AND, IN SO DOING, BRAINWASHES THE TOWN AND GIVES JAPAN ITS FIRST FOOTHOLD IN THE UNITED STATES. UNSOLICITED BY PRESIDENT ROOSEVELT, SCHWERDLOFF ALSO PRODUCED *KRAUTHEADS,* A MOVIE HE HOPED WOULD SHOW—AND IT DID—THAT SCHWERDLOFF, IN SPITE OF HIS NAME, HATED THE GERMANS AS MUCH AS EVERYBODY ELSE DID.

LIKE ALL STUDIOS, THE MR. SCHWERDLOFF STUDIO HAD ITS "B" PICTURES AS WELL. MOST SUCCESSFUL AMONG THESE WERE THE "MEL THE TROUT" SERIES, ABOUT A TROUT WHO SAVES A BOY AND HIS FAMILY AND, ONCE, A WHOLE TOWN, BY ALERTING THEM TO THE DANGERS OF LIFE IN THE MOUNTAINS; AND THE "BIG DWAYNE" SERIES, STARRING EX-OLYMPIC SHOTPUTTER KEVIN BLONK, WHO SAVES PEOPLE BY THROWING THINGS.

MUSICALS WERE POPULAR IN THE THIRTIES AND FORTIES, BUT THE MR. SCHWERDLOFF STUDIO MADE ONLY TWO. MR. SCHWERDLOFF HATED MUSICALS. "ANYTHING WORTH SINGING IS WORTH SAYING," HE USED TO SAY. IT WASN'T JUST SINGING MR. SCHWERDLOFF HATED. HE ONCE TOLD HIS SECRETARY, ABILENE KRONENBERG, "STOP THAT HUMMING—I HATE MUSIC!" THOUGH MR. SCHWERDLOFF HATED THE TWO MUSICALS, *SING-A-LING* AND *SHORE LEAVE,* THEY WERE IMMENSELY SUCCESSFUL AT THE BOX OFFICE.

THESE WERE NOT ONLY GOOD PROFESSIONAL YEARS FOR SCHWERDLOFF. IN 1938 HIS ONLY SON WAS BORN: HIS PRIDE AND JOY, X.Y. SCHWERDLOFF, JR., LATER NICKNAMED BUCKY AFTER HIS TEETH. X.Y. HAD TWO DAUGHTERS—JULIA AND AMELIA—AND HE LIKED THEM ALL RIGHT BUT HE HAD ALWAYS WANTED A BOY. THE DAY BUCKY WAS BORN, SCHWERDLOFF WAS SO HAPPY HE GAVE EVERYONE AT THE STUDIO A SEVEN-POUND-THREE-OUNCE PASTRY REPLICA OF THE INFANT. THE PASTRIES WERE DESIGNED BY JEAN PAUL OF LE CIRQUE AND DR. PENN, BUCKY'S PEDIATRICIAN. SCHWERD-LOFF WOULD GIVE THIS GIFT EVERY YEAR TO HIS EMPLOYEES ON BUCKY'S BIRTHDAY. AS BUCKY GREW BIGGER, SO DID THE PASTRIES.

THESE YEARS, FROM 1935 TO 1945, WERE THE HEYDAY OF THE MR. SCHWERDLOFF STUDIO. IN LARGE PART THIS WAS DUE TO THE FAMILY ATMOSPHERE X.Y. SCHWERDLOFF FOSTERED. CONCERNED THAT HIS STARS NOT STRAY DOWN THE WAYWARD PATH OF DRUG AND DRINK THAT SO MANY OTHERS HAD FOLLOWED, SCHWERDLOFF SOUGHT ACTIVELY TO MOLD THEIR CHARACTERS AND INSTILL IN THEM A SENSE OF RESPONSIBILITY AND SELF-WORTH. NO STAR WAS EVER GIVEN A RAISE SIMPLY BECAUSE HE OR SHE WAS POPULAR AT THE BOX OFFICE. THE RAISE HAD TO BE EARNED. TO GET HER $2,500 A WEEK RAISE, LILLIAN GISH HAD TO SWEEP OUT THE GARAGE FOR A MONTH.

SCHWERDLOFF RAN THE STUDIO WITH AN IRON HAND AND HIS TEMPER WAS LEGENDARY, BUT HE GUIDED THE STUDIO THROUGH FORTY-EIGHT PROFITABLE YEARS (ONLY 1960 SHOWED A LOSS).

SCHWERDLOFF WAS STILL AT WORK WHEN HE DIED IN 1961. HE DIED OF A HEART ATTACK WHEN HIS FILM ABOUT A LIVESTOCK FARMER DEALING WITH A FLOOD, BAY OF PIGS, OPENED THE SAME DAY THAT THE UNITED STATES LEARNED IT HAD SUFFERED AN UN-PARALLELED MILITARY HUMILIATION IN CUBAN WATERS. MISTAKING NEWS REPORTS OF THE DISASTER FOR REVIEWS OF HIS FILM, SCHWERD-LOFF WAS APPALLED WHEN HE SAW THE HEADLINE OF THAT MORN-ING'S LOS ANGELES TIMES: "BAY OF PIGS DISGRACES U.S." WHEN HE READ THAT PRESIDENT KENNEDY WOULD ADDRESS THE NATION ON THE SUBJECT THAT NIGHT, SCHWERDLOFF'S HEART STOPPED FOREVER.

FIRSTS AT THE MR. SCHWERDLOFF STUDIO

• First studio to pan to a fireplace while characters made love (*The Rapscallion from Bavaria*, 1923, silent).

• First studio to drop major characters from a classic and mangle the ending (*There's No Place Like Home*, adapted from Charles Dickens's *Bleak House*, 1924, silent).

• First studio to do a movie with British accents (*Simon the Orphan Boy*, 1929).

• First studio to have a movie in which a woman disguises herself as a man and then has to smoke a cigar and nearly chokes to death (*Let's Play Golf*, 1933).

• First and only studio to use a chain letter to promote a movie (*The Story of the Pony Express*, 1953, Cinemascope).

• First studio to release a movie that was not in Swedish that had a clock ticking so loudly you could not hear the characters talking (*Paranoia*, 1958).

ELIZABETH TAYLOR, actress

Mr. Schwerdloff was the first producer I worked for in Hollywood. I was eight when I started working for him. My first picture was *The Kissing Cousin* with Roddy McDowall. Mr. Schwerdloff came to the set at least once a day to see how the film was progressing. He took an interest in all the pictures filmed at his studio. Sometimes, at the end of the day, if he thought I wasn't doing my best, he'd take me out behind Tulip Street on the Olde New Orleans set where we filmed the "Happy Harts" series and he would wallop me with his belt. Other times, if I was feeling sick, he'd come over to the house and sit on the edge of my bed and hit me with a hairbrush. He was like a father to me.

LIZA MINNELLI, actress

Momma worked there once on a picture and Papa came over to direct. Momma and Papa were married then. I remember coming to the set with Momma's Momma, Gromma, and Momma's Papa, Groppa, and Groppa's Papa, Great-Groppa. Someone gave me a lollipop. I think it was Francis Ford Coppola's papa, Papa Coppola. I know it wasn't Mr. Schwerdloff. I don't remember Mr. Schwerdloff.

PETER PERRY, assistant to Mr. Schwerdloff, 1919–1946

I guess what people remember most about Mr. Schwerdloff was his wit. Oh, God, oh, God, I remember when he told Ann Miller, "Your mouth is so big, I can't look at it, get off my lot and don't stop driving till you're out of gas."

Some people said he was malicious but I never saw that side of him.

ABILENE MOREDOCK, secretary to Mr. Schwerdloff, 1920–1960

I worked for Mr. Schwerdloff for forty years, God knows why. He was a tyrant, though I will say, whenever he yelled at me, he always used my name. You can't deny he had manners.

Here's an example of a day I hated: Mr. Schwerdloff hated when a contract was stapled because it made it harder for him to sneak in an extra page, which was something he liked to do when he wanted to take someone's rights away without them knowing it. So, one day, God knows why, I forgot and stapled a contract instead of using a paper clip. It wasn't two seconds later and he was at my desk. He grabbed my stapler and pulled the base back. He said, "How many times have I told you, Mrs. Moredock . . ." and then on every syllable he fired a staple at me: *"We do not sta-ple con-tracts!"* I have never been so humiliated in my life. None of the staples stuck—don't ask me why, he was firing from close enough—but when I got home that night my husband asked me if I had prickly heat.

There were only two times I ever saw Mr. Schwerdloff act like a human being. Those were the times his little boy came to the office. Mr. Schwerdloff carried him on his shoulders, pushed him around in his chair, they fed the ducks in the studio pond. The only times I ever saw him laugh were with Bucky.

WALTER SCHWERDLOFF, nephew of X.Y. Schwerdloff

Uncle X. started out in rugs. That was our family's business back in Brooklyn. He and Dad were working in the shop one day and some guy from a moving-picture company needed a rug pad to block out some stray light and, well, before you knew it, Uncle X. was in the movie business!

He formed a small company with the rug business as collateral and began producing movies.

PAULINE KAEL, film critic

At a recent Schwerdloff Studio retrospective, my companion remarked to me that he didn't think any studio ever used as many rugs in its movies as the Schwerdloff Studio did. He was right; it was a real Rug-Out.

Schwerdloff, a second generation immigrant, always felt guilty about having done so well in the movies while his family struggled with their rug business. To make it up to them, Schwerdloff bought hundreds of rugs from them for each picture and lavishly decorated each set with the rugs whether the set needed one or not.

ALFRED HITCHCOCK, director (from his article "Deepest, Darkest Hollywood," from *Arts, Lettres, Spectacles*, June 1, 1960)

Originally, I was to direct my famous picture *Lifeboat* for the Mr. Schwerdloff Studio, but was unable to do so because of an altercation I had with the producer, Mr. X.Y. Schwerdloff. Mr. Schwerdloff wanted the lifeboat to be carpeted with a gaily colored scatter rug. When I submitted that a scatter rug on a lifeboat was unrealistic, Mr. Schwerdloff replied, "And I suppose it's realistic that people are on a lifeboat for five days and no one ever has to go to the bathroom!"

WALTER SCHWERDLOFF, nephew of X.Y. Schwerdloff

In those days, you know, when movies were new, people would see anything. Uncle X. used to say that if it was terrible they'd only see it three times. One of Uncle X.'s first movies was called *Stripping the Bed*. It was about three minutes long. My mom starred in it. She stripped the bed. It only took her about two minutes, so a lot of the movie was of the bed itself. Of its type, it's good. Very realistic.

It was so magic. Before, if you wanted to see a bed stripped, you had to go to people's houses. You had to go to people's bedrooms. You had to go to people's beds. Not after the movies. Not after *Stripping the Bed*. From then on, the bed came to you. We all saw it over and over. It's really the whole idea behind *Jules and Jim*.

STAN GILLIES, head of business affairs at the Mr. Schwerdloff Studio, 1935–1961

I started at Schwerdloff in 1935. I handled petty cash for *Young Charlemagne*. Of all my films, I'm proudest of *Young Charlemagne*. Though it won more Academy Award nominations than any other film that year, it didn't do much box office, but still, true movies like that make history really sink in. To this day, I can still see Mickey Rooney skipping rocks and singing about how he wanted to be the first Frankish emperor crowned by the Pope.

There wasn't one year we were in the red except '60. That was the year we put out our big Bible epic, *They Bring First the Fruit*.* As it turned out, that was $10.6 million we could've torn up and thrown in the trash.

From a business-affairs point of view, that year, '60, was our worst. But from an overall point of view, '52 was worse. That was when Mr. Schwerdloff was called before the House Un-American Activities Committee.

They Bring First the Fruit (1960), Victor Mature, Anne Baxter, Leslie Caron.

17

D. EDWARD KELLEY, attorney

I counseled Mr. Schwerdloff before he spoke to the committee. He was very upset, very nervous. It was the only time I ever saw him nervous. He was afraid he'd lose the studio. Afterward, people accused him of being spineless and I guess you'd have to say he *was* spineless, but he was spineless in that forceful way of his.

TRANSCRIPT OF HUAC HEARING: DEFENDANT, X.Y. SCHWERDLOFF,
APRIL 4, 1952

SENATOR JOHN S. WOOD: Mr. Schwerdloff, are you familiar with a film called *It's a Girl!*?

X. Y. SCHWERDLOFF: No, sir.

WOOD: You're not familiar with the film *It's a Girl!*?

SCHWERDLOFF: No, sir.

WOOD: *It's a Girl!* was released by your studio in 1943.

SCHWERDLOFF: Well . . .

WOOD: And because of the shortage of manpower during the war, you personally produced the film.

SCHWERDLOFF: Oh! *It's a Girl!* I thought you were saying *It's a Gorilla!*

WOOD: No, sir. *It's a Girl!*

SCHWERDLOFF: Oh, yes. *It's a Girl!*

18

WOOD: You know *It's a Girl!*?

SCHWERDLOFF: I know *It's a Girl!* I do not know *It's a Gorilla!*

WOOD: No, sir. *It's a Girl!* Now are you aware that in your film *It's a Girl!*, the hero moves *east* three times? *East*, not west, as in where the United States is, but *east*, as in the *Eastern* Bloc of Communist countries. Are you aware that the hero of *It's a Girl!* moves *east* three times?

SCHWERDLOFF: Well, sir, I personally produced the film. I should think I'd know what's in it.

WOOD: Now if you were traveling east, sir, and you left this great country and you kept traveling east, what country would you end up in?

SCHWERDLOFF: England.

WOOD: Well, yes, sir, but further east than that. Go further east.

SCHWERDLOFF: Oh, Senator Wood, I really don't know geography.

WOOD: Think about it. It's a big country. If you were in England and you took a giant leap east, over all those little countries, what big country would you land in?

SCHWERDLOFF: Uh . . . Chile?

D. EDWARD KELLEY, attorney

Most of the hearing was about geography. Eventually the committee made clear its objections to the film, pointing out the subversive implications of traveling east. Schwerdloff apologized. He said he wasn't aware that there was any symbolism in the movie, that he would sacrifice his own wife for this country, and that, if it would make the committee feel better, he would eat the film. They took a vote and decided it would make them feel better. He ate the film.

JOHN FORD (from the John Ford interview, "And Then I Made . . ." in *Film Comment,* September 25, 1969

The fifties were hard on X.Y. It wasn't just the McCarthy thing. Television was eating up the business, and while the other studios made up for their losses by selling their films to TV, X.Y. refused. He said he'd rather eat them. Then there was that big Bible thing he did, the *Fruit* thing.* He nearly lost his shirt on that. And then *Pigs,* our picture, *Bay of Pigs,* went over budget. And just speaking of that, I'd tell anybody making a pig picture today, they might as well stick another million on the budget right away—and they'd better not think they can get around it using hogs, either—there's no working with swine. Period.

Anyway, *Pigs* came in finally at $11.5 million—astronomical in those days, easily the most expensive picture of the year. But, goddamn, if it wasn't a corker! We knew we had a classic. When Hank Fonda looked out over his farm and saw that the pigs he'd worked so hard to get were floating across the fields in the flood, and then he swims out to save the special one, the pregnant one— well, even the crew went weepy.

X.Y. was thrilled because he needed something big. The way things had stacked up that year, if *Pigs* lost money, X.Y. would've been down two years in a row and that was too much for his ego to take—he hated failure. Also, he was beginning his sixth decade in the movie

They Bring First the Fruit (1960), Victor Mature, Anne Baxter, Leslie Caron.

business and he didn't want to be thought of as a relic. He had to show he still knew how to make pictures, goddammit! He had so much riding on that film! So, when he saw the headlines that day about the Bay of Pigs and thought they were the reviews, and then he saw the part about the president being upset and the United States embarrassing itself in front of the whole world—well, it was too much for him. His heart gave out.

The sad thing is he could've been saved. Letty, his wife, waited five hours before calling the ambulance. She saw him in the driveway where he'd gone to get the morning paper. He'd collapsed face down onto the gravel and Letty figured he'd just gone back to sleep. It wasn't until she tried to back the car out on her way to lunch and couldn't get him to move that she suspected something was wrong.

Poor Letty, it didn't get any better for her after that.

AMELIA SCHWERDLOFF DUFFEE, daughter of X.Y. Schwerdloff

My first kid died at her fourth birthday party, before the clown came. My husband was shot in the mouth at LaGuardia Airport trying to get a cab. But nothing—zip, zero, nada—can compare to the day that Dad's will was read.

D. EDWARD KELLEY, attorney

I knew there'd be an uproar when I read the will. I begged X.Y. not to put the paragraph in but he was adamant. I knew Mrs. Schwerdloff would be shocked. I knew she would feel sadness. I knew she would feel pain. Admitting that, however, I never imagined that she would take it the way she did.

Apparently, Mrs. Schwerdloff had not known that for the last forty-five years of her marriage, X.Y. had been seeing another woman, and the will, paragraph 3 in particular, made that sad fact quite clear.

PARAGRAPH 3, FROM THE LAST WILL AND TESTAMENT OF X.Y. SCHWERDLOFF

. . . And to Doreen Barker, my most beloved companion of these last forty-five years, I leave the beautiful cluster ring with the stunning sapphire center that I gave to my wife at our wedding 45 or 46 years ago. The ring can be located on my wife's third finger and may need to be cut off.

D. EDWARD KELLEY, attorney

This was a stressful moment for Mrs. Schwerdloff and matters were not made easier when Doreen cried, "This is the happiest day of my life!" It seemed X.Y. had promised that they would be married someday and now she was getting her wish. Doreen moved quickly to gain possession of the ring, but Mrs. Schwerdloff obstructed her access. Eventually, Doreen jumped on her and tried to chew it off but she split her lip and had to sit back.

Somehow the news about Doreen got out, and when the obits appeared, she was mentioned.

OBITUARY, EXCERPTED FROM THE *LOS ANGELES TIMES*, APRIL 19, 1963

. . . Mr. Schwerdloff is survived by his wife of 45 years; his two daughters, Julia Bush and Amelia Duffee; and his one son, X.Y. Schwerdloff, Jr. (Bucky). After his death, Schwerdloff became engaged to be married to Miss Doreen Barker of Topanga Park, California. No date has been set. A memorial service will be held this Friday at 1:30 at Forest Lawn.

JULIA SCHWERDLOFF BUSH, daughter of X.Y. Schwerdloff

The worst part of the funeral for me was seeing Daddy. Oh, it was just so terrible. Mother asked if she could dress him and we all thought, *Well, sure, good idea!* You know, we were hoping it would be cathartic for her. But Mother was still upset about the ring, and when we got to the funeral, well, we saw right away we had made the wrong decision. I'm sorry to say Mother could be very vindictive. She had dressed Daddy in a red satin cocktail dress, off the shoulder, with some flounce around the middle, and then—oh, I still shudder when I think of it: she announced to everyone that it was Daddy's wish to be dressed in something he liked to wear around the house. Oh, I forgot—there were little ribbons in his hair. Oh, dear!

As if this weren't enough, that awful woman, Doreen, showed up in the middle of the service. She was in a wedding dress and she marched right up that . . . kind of aisle and she went over to Daddy and took a gun out and said to Mother, "Give me that ring or I'll shoot him!" It's sad what some people will do to get married. But then, thank God, that huge man that played in all those awful "Big Dwayne" movies stood up and threw a prayer book at her. He knocked her out, just as Rabbi Weiss was concluding his eulogy. Rabbi Weiss said, "X.Y. Schwerdloff was a great man and a strong man and, from the looks of him, a cute man."

Daddy's death affected Bucky the most. The burial was private, so, after everyone left the funeral parlor and the men were going to move the body, Bucky broke down. He asked if he could be alone with Daddy for a little while. He said, "I'm sorry but I guess I'm just sensitive to death." Of course we let him stay.

After a little bit, I looked back in. Bucky was holding a mirror up to Daddy's mouth.

When I looked in a little later, Bucky was talking to Daddy. He was telling Daddy not to worry, that he'd take care of the family and make sure that we were all provided for.

Bucky sat with Daddy all afternoon and would've stayed all night but finally I came in and told him, "I'm sorry, we have to bury Daddy. It's getting dark." He didn't want to leave but Meelie, that's my older sister, Amelia, Meelie told him it was against the law to bury people after dark, so Bucky agreed. He said, "I don't want Daddy to break the law." Before we closed the coffin, Bucky asked if he could have something to remember Daddy by. Isn't that sweet? We said of course. He took one of the little ribbons out of Daddy's hair.

At dinner that night, Bucky told us that even though Daddy was dead, Bucky was not going to drop the "Jr." from his name. He said that although his own achievements would probably far surpass Daddy's, he wanted people to know where he came from.

Poor Bucky.

CHAPTER 2

FADE OUT: MR. SCHWERDLOFF

BARBRA STREISAND, actress

In 1961, I was living over a fish restaurant and singing at the Bon Soir, a club on West Eighth. I was the freshest thing anyone had ever seen. People still talk about it. Look at us—we're still talking about it.

So some talent guy from the Schwerdloff Studio heard me sing. He said I had the most beautiful voice he'd ever heard. He wanted me to audition for Schwerdloff. He said he'd fly me out to Hollywood first class. He said "first class" like it was some honor. Big deal, I thought, that's how they send mail. He said he'd arrange to have a limo pick me up at the airport. He said he'd put me up at the Beverly Wilshire. *Me* fly to Hollywood, *me* find the limo, *me* stay at the Beverly Wilshire, *me* audition. That's the way they treat you before you're big—like a piece of meat.

So Monday I fly out. I hate flying because no matter how many times you tell the girl to give you another tray of food, she won't. So I get there and go to my suite. I'd never seen better but I knew there *was* better, so I made them give me another suite. They gave me the best they had. I knew there were better suites than that, but I was too tired to switch hotels.

The next day I went to the studio. Some nothing met me at the gates and said, "I'm sorry to have to tell you this, Miss Streisand, but we'll have to postpone your audition. Mr. Schwerdloff passed away this morning. . . ." Blah-blah-blah . . .

I'd had enough. "You coulda told me this yesterday," I said, "before I'd flown all the way out here!"

I waited for months to hear from them. That studio was a mess after he died.

. . .

ANDREW GUNDLACH WAS APPOINTED TO RUN THE STUDIO AFTER MR. SCHWERDLOFF'S DEATH AND HELD THAT POSITION UNTIL 1966. THOUGH GUNDLACH CONSISTENTLY MANAGED TO TURN A PROFIT IN AN ERA WHEN MOST STUDIOS WERE FALTERING, HIS TYRANNICAL PERSONALITY ALIENATED EVERY SINGLE PERSON WITH WHOM HE CAME IN CONTACT. FINALLY, AFTER FIVE TURBULENT YEARS, GUNDLACH RESIGNED. THERE WERE RUMORS THAT GUNDLACH WAS FORCED OUT, BUT NOTHING IS KNOWN FOR SURE. THE BOARD RELEASED ONLY THIS STATEMENT: "UNDER THE GUIDANCE OF ANDREW GUNDLACH, THE MR. SCHWERDLOFF STUDIO HAS RELEASED SOME FINE MOTION PICTURES, BUT WE HATE HIS GUTS."

BY 1966, THE MR. SCHWERDLOFF STUDIO'S RELATIONSHIP WITH THE HOLLYWOOD CREATIVE COMMUNITY WAS AT AN ALL-TIME LOW. TO GET OUT OF ACCEPTING AN ASSIGNMENT AT THE STUDIO, MANY ACTORS SERVED IN VIETNAM. IN AN EFFORT TO REGAIN ITS PRESTIGIOUS POSITION AMONG THE STUDIOS, THE MR. SCHWERDLOFF BOARD APPOINTED AS PRESIDENT BANNET RICHARDS, THE ACADEMY AWARD WINNING PRODUCER KNOWN FOR HIS LAVISH MUSICALS (*HIP, HIP, HOORAY!*, *BON VOYAGE!*, *STANDING ROOM ONLY!*). RICH-

ARDS PROMISED TO MAKE THE STUDIO A PLACE "WHERE ARTISTS WOULD WANT TO WORK AGAIN."

THOUGH RICHARDS DID INDEED GET SOME OF HOLLYWOOD'S MOST POPULAR ARTISTS TO WORK AT THE STUDIO AGAIN, HE UNLUCKILY GOT SOME OF THEIR LEAST POPULAR WORK. THE STUDIO BEGAN LOSING MONEY. MAJOR MONEY LOSERS IN THE FIRST YEAR INCLUDED: *FLIBBERTYGIBBIT,* A FAMILY MUSICAL ABOUT A POOR FAMILY AND THEIR FLYING HOUSE, STARRING DICK VAN DYKE AND FLORENCE HENDERSON ($7.2 MILLION); *SOMEPLACE NOT SO COLD,* THE DAVID LEAN EPIC ABOUT LEIF ERICSON, STARRING KEIR DULLEA ($9.6 MILLION); AND *BIG DEAL,* THE FOUR-HOUR ALL-STAR DRAMATIZATION OF THE LOUISIANA PURCHASE ($11.9 MILLION).

BY 1969, RICHARDS'S FAILURES HAD COST THE STUDIO $90 MILLION. HE LEARNED OF HIS FIRING ON HIS SIXTIETH BIRTHDAY WHEN MESSENGERS BROUGHT HIM A SEVEN-LAYER ANGEL FOOD CAKE WITH PINK ICING THAT READ, "WE'RE SORRY BUT WE HAVE TO LET YOU GO." THE BOARD LIKED RICHARDS AND WANTED TO TELL HIM ABOUT HIS DISMISSAL IN AS PLEASANT A WAY AS POSSIBLE.

RICHARDS WAS REPLACED BY ED KLOMAN, A LAWYER, JUST TWO DAYS BEFORE THE ANNUAL STOCKHOLDERS' MEETING. AT THE MEETING, KLOMAN CHARMED THOSE PRESENT WITH HIS REMARKS.

FROM "A WORD FROM THE PRESIDENT" BY ED KLOMAN, IN THE ANNUAL STOCKHOLDERS' MEETING REPORT, FEBRUARY 12, 1980

In every year, there are negatives and positives. This year our feature film division lost $66 million. Each of the twelve films we released lost all the money we put into them. Our Christmas film, *To Mercury and Back,* was the phenomenal failure of the decade. More Americans have been to Mercury than have been to *To Mercury and Back.* The television division reports an unheard-of loss of $44 million.

On the positive side. People never complain about our returning their calls. In every part of the creative community, including Europe, there is a sense of enthusiasm about our performance in this area.

Secondly, as the studio farthest from Los Angeles, we suffer less from the smog, making the studio an attractive arena in which to work during an age when people are growing increasingly conscious of their breathing needs. Scientists say that by the year 2060, MGM and Paramount will be so covered with smog that they will be uninhabitable if they do not move. Thus, two of our major competitors will be wiped out.

Thirdly, the Olympics were this year and the United States did very well. That is something we can all be proud of, especially those of us who work for a studio like ours, situated in California, a state that produced so many fine swimmers. . . .

. . .

KLOMAN REMAINED AT THE MR. SCHWERDLOFF STUDIO FOR EIGHTEEN MONTHS, DURING WHICH THE STUDIO CONTINUED ITS DOWNWARD COURSE. IN 1982, REED RAYMAN WAS HIRED TO REPLACE KLOMAN. RAYMAN WAS A FAMILIAR FIGURE IN HOLLYWOOD. HE HAD HEADED SEVERAL MAJOR STUDIOS, SOMETIMES TWICE, THOUGH NEVER PROFITABLY. HE CONTINUED TO LOSE MONEY.

SINCE X.Y. SCHWERDLOFF'S DEATH AND THE INSTITUTIONALIZATION OF MRS. SCHWERDLOFF, CONTROLLING INTEREST IN THE STUDIO WAS HELD BY SCHWERDLOFF'S CHILDREN. THE CHILDREN, HOWEVER, PAID LITTLE ATTENTION TO THE AFFAIRS OF THE STUDIO, HAVING PROMINENT CAREERS OF THEIR OWN: JULIA SCHWERDLOFF BUSH IS AN ECONOMIST AT THE WORLD BANK; AMELIA SCHWERDLOFF DUFFEE IS THE NAVY'S FIRST WOMAN ADMIRAL; AND BUCKY SCHWERDLOFF RUNS TWO PRIVATE BUSINESSES. BUT BY 1982, THE STUDIO HAD LOST SO MUCH MONEY THAT THE SCHWERDLOFFS WERE REQUIRED TO TAKE ACTION.

JULIA SCHWERDLOFF BUSH

None of us had anything to do with the studio when we were growing up. Daddy wanted us to lead normal lives and he was very strict about our staying away from the studio. The guards had orders to shoot if we came to the gates. Just warning shots—Daddy would never hurt us.

After Daddy's death and then Mother's being institutionalized—oh, that's so sad that someone who likes to drive as much as Mother does has to be institutionalized—we didn't really keep up with the studio, even though we were the major stockholders. Daddy had set up a very generous trust so that none of us would ever have to worry about money. Wasn't that sweet? And we were all so busy with our work, and we'd all moved east, that the studio just seemed far away. Actually, Bucky hadn't moved east—he lived right there.

But by 1982, it had become clear that the studio was in just a . . . oh, a, well, just a hopeless financial mess. The banks had refused to lend the studio any more money and they wanted to settle the debts the studio had. Meelie and I decided to shut the studio down and sell the assets. I thought we should send someone from the family to tell everyone at the studio. It just seemed like the only decent thing to do since so many of the people had worked there so long. We decided to send Bucky.

AMELIA SCHWERDLOFF DUFFEE

I knew we never should've sent Buck. As sure as I'm sitting here, I knew it. I told Julia, "Listen up. Buck's a poor choice for this job," but she couldn't see a problem with it. She said, "All he has to do is say six words: 'I'm sorry we're closing the studio down.' " She even wrote it down for him. How could he possibly mess up?, she asked. "Take it from me," I said, "he will." Messing up is the one area where Buck shows any ingenuity.

CHAPTER 3

CLOSE-UP: BUCKY SCHWERDLOFF

JULIA SCHWERDLOFF BUSH

I wish we could do it all over again and let Bucky grow up like any other boy. Bucky was the youngest and I guess we just felt protective of him, especially Daddy.

Daddy didn't get to see Bucky very much because he was so busy at the studio, but every now and then, he'd leave work early to spend time with him.

I remember the time Daddy brought Bucky home a bike. He was going to teach Bucky how to ride it. Bucky was so excited. He got right on the bike and Daddy pushed him down the road. Daddy said, "I'm going to let go now, I'm going to let go!"

Bucky said, "Okay!"

The second Daddy let go, Bucky fell and started to cry. Daddy asked Mother what Bucky was doing. This was the first time he'd ever seen Bucky cry—as I say, he was home so rarely. Mother said that Bucky was just crying and Daddy said, "Haven't we made him happy?"

Bucky kept crying and crying. Daddy said that he

couldn't stand it another second. Mother should make Bucky stop it right away. Mother told him that Bucky would get over it, but that wasn't good enough for Daddy.

That night Daddy called me and Meelie into his room and told us that seeing Bucky so upset by this failure had been the most heartbreaking experience of Daddy's life. You should remember that Daddy never showed his emotions—except for rage—so when he told us how much this had upset him, it was so touching. Then he told us he would see to it that Bucky was never disappointed again.

The next day, Daddy had two men from the studio run alongside of Bucky to prop him up when he rode his bike. For ten years, for as long as Bucky rode a bike, Mr. Bash and Mr. Neely ran alongside of him. Bucky never figured out why they were there. He just thought they liked his company.

He was a good man, Dad, but when it came to Buck, he was soft. Like: Buck came home after the first day of first grade, bawling because the teacher said he held the pencil incorrectly. So, Dad bought the school. He told the teachers that from that point on if Buck couldn't understand something right away, they should apologize to Buck and announce to the other kids that they were wrong and that Buck was right.

TEDDY STUART, former classmate of Bucky Schwerdloff

I was in class with Bucky for five years and I'm still not over it. He thought that when you added two numbers, you just put them together. Two plus four is twenty-four, six plus nine is sixty-nine, and so on. And because he thought it, that's what we were taught. Two plus four is twenty-four! That *is* wrong, isn't it?

Because of Bucky, I didn't get an education. But he was such a sad character, it's hard to hold that against him. When I think of the day we had that substitute teacher, poor old Mrs. Rucker, who didn't know the rules about Bucky and kept saying that he was wrong when he said that Alexander Graham Bell invented the belt, I have to pity Bucky. He turned beet red and then started yanking his hair. His jaw locked. Then he turned purple. We were all so scared. Mrs. Rucker had to call an ambulance.

DR. JIM WITKIN, shock specialist, Beverly Hills Hospital

The Schwerdloff boy was in a coma by the time they got him to the hospital. We tried everything but we couldn't bring him out of it. Nothing worked until some teacher, I think, some woman from his school came in and whispered in his ear, "I'm sorry, you were right." Suddenly he sat up and was as good as new.

AMELIA SCHWERDLOFF DUFFEE

It's hard to know if Buck was a born idiot or if we made him an idiot, but there's no doubt he *is* an idiot.

Now, when Dad died, Julia and I had to figure out what to do about Buck. Buck was twenty-three and I thought it was time he knew he was an idiot. I wanted to tell him he was an idiot but Julia begged me to keep quiet. I also wanted to stop subsidizing those idiot businesses of his. Dad had been secretly underwriting Buck's two businesses so Buck wouldn't find out he was a business idiot. Julia said, "We can't cut him off yet. He's not ready." As if Buck'd ever be ready for business!

I mean, listen up, Buck had a business that sold something he'd invented called Straight Rope. The way he explained it to me was, "You know, Meelie, when you tie your boat up to the dock and the boat will bang against the dock? I hate that!" He saw it as the rope's fault. So he dreamed up this thing called Straight Rope which was just rope that wouldn't bend. When I pointed out that this was the exact same thing as a pole, he very patiently said, "No, Meelie"—he's always patient with other people when he's wrong—"a pole has a flag on it!" Of course, in a way, it was different than a pole: it snapped in half under the slightest pressure. This didn't bother him, though. "Then people will need more!"*

*Between the years 1951 and 1986, X.Y. Schwerdloff, and then the Schwerdloff sisters, spent over $33 million secretly underwriting Bucky Schwerdloff's two businesses.

Buck also had a chain of highway restaurants called Squash-and-Drive because Buck noticed that on long drives there was no place to get a good baked winter squash, which was a dish we all loved at the house. That's Buck for you—he sees a void and he jumps into it!

BUCKY SCHWERDLOFF

Let me tell you something about me. I'm the kind of man—here's who I am. When I see a problem, I don't run away from it, I run *toward* it. Straight into it if I have to. I'm not cautious. I like to take risks. Taking risks is the only way to succeed and succeeding is the only way to grow.

So when the girls called me and asked me to do what had to be done at the studio, I said I would. I knew it would mean a lot of technical business stuff, and I like to shield them from that sort of thing. Besides, they were busy with their homes, their shopping, their . . . faces, I guess, and also, they have jobs. They work very hard at their jobs.

JULIA SCHWERDLOFF BUSH

Bucky always tells us how proud he is of us for working, but, well, really I don't think he understands what we do. The day I told him I'd gotten the job at the World Bank, he said, "Well, that's great, but, you know, if you wanted, I could pull a few strings and try to get you a job at a bank with a few more branches."

Meelie was the first woman admiral. When Alene Duerk was appointed as the second, Bucky was very upset. He thought they'd hired her because Meelie wasn't getting her work done. He wasn't trying to be cruel. He could never be cruel. He just didn't understand.

BUCKY SCHWERDLOFF

Truth be told, when the girls asked me to close the studio, it was an inconvenient time for me. We were beginning a two-week experiment in the Squash-and-Drive where we used paper pans, an idea of mine to help us cut our costs.* But when your sisters call, it's hard to say no.

· · ·

ON OCTOBER 1, 1982, BUCKY SCHWERDLOFF FLEW TO HOLLYWOOD AND MET WITH REED RAYMAN, THEN HEAD OF PRODUCTION AT THE MR. SCHWERDLOFF STUDIO.

*Over the two-week period, this resulted in nearly eighty fires and $10 million worth of damage.

When I went to lunch with Bucky, I wore a dark suit. I thought a dark suit said, "I know the studio lost $23.5 million in the third quarter, but, for God's sake, don't do anything rash such as, say, for instance, firing me." When Bucky picked me up, he was wearing a plaid suit. That made me nervous—I can never tell what plaid is saying. But then Bucky drove us to a cheap Mexican restaurant called Adios Amigos and I got the idea.

I sat closest to the door and I never put my fork down because I've noticed that people are less inclined to fire you if they have to walk by you when you're holding a fork. But then, wouldn't you know it, a waitress brushed up against me and I dropped my fork. I quickly bent over to pick it up. Not quick enough. Sure enough, Bucky said he was letting me go. And he wasn't just letting me go, he was closing the whole studio down. This was a relief—I hate to be the only one who's fired. But still, I begged him to keep the studio open. I said to him, "It seems to me that throwing in the towel and admitting failure, isn't— well, I can't see your father doing it." This seemed to get him.

Bucky stared at the table for a long time, chewing on the corner of his napkin. I chewed on mine too, hoping it would make him feel closer to me. But then he said, "No, I've got to close it. I'm sorry."

BUCKY SCHWERDLOFF

Reed left before I did. I wanted to sit with my coffee and think things over. I thought about Dad and how sad he'd have been that we were selling the studio.

As I drank my coffee, I noticed this guy next to me. He had taken a bag out of his pocket. It was filled with dirt. He was sprinkling it over his food. I asked him what he was doing and he said that he was from the Hermits from Christ, some religious group. I could tell he was religious even before he put dirt on his food. He was wearing that monk dress.

• • •

THE MONK WAS FRIAR CURRIE. THE RELIGIOUS ORDER HE BELONGED TO WAS THE HERMITS *OF* CHRIST, A RELIGIOUS FRATERNITY BASED IN NORTHERN CALIFORNIA. THE HERMITS WERE FOUNDED IN 1854 BY FLANN WASHBURN WHEN WASHBURN AND HIS FOLLOWERS SPLIT FROM THE JESUITS OVER A DISPUTE ABOUT EVERYTHING.

ORIGINALLY CALLED THE COMMUNITARIANS OF CHRIST, THE GROUP ESTABLISHED ITSELF IN ABINGTON, PENNSYLVANIA. THE COMMUNITARIANS BELIEVED THAT A PERSON'S BEHAVIOR IN THIS LIFE DETERMINED WHETHER HE WOULD GO TO HEAVEN. WASHBURN BELIEVED THAT ALL PEOPLE WOULD GO TO HEAVEN IF THEY ACCEPTED THE TEACHINGS OF GOD AS SET FORTH IN THE BIBLE. FOR THAT REASON, THE GROUP DEDICATED ITSELF TO "LIVING AMONGST THE PEOPLE AND NOT APART FROM THEM, SPREADING THE WORD OF THE LORD TO OUR NEIGHBORS, NOT ONLY TO OURSELVES, AND

HELPING TO FOSTER A COMMUNITY WHERE PEOPLE OF ALL FAITHS CAN LIVE IN PEACE AND UNDERSTANDING TOGETHER."

THE COMMUNITARIANS DID NOT CALL ABINGTON, PENNSYLVANIA, HOME FOR LONG. AFTER TWO WEEKS THEY LEFT, TIRED OF HAVING THEIR ROBES RIDICULED BY THE TOWNSPEOPLE.

THE COMMUNITARIANS MOVED TO LISHVILLE, WEST VIRGINIA, BUT LEFT A FEW DAYS LATER BECAUSE THE VILLAGERS REFUSED TO STOP PULLING THEIR FRONTLOCKS, THE LOCK OF HAIR THAT HUNG DOWN THE CENTER OF THEIR FACES. THE COMMUNITARIANS WERE NOT ALLOWED TO CUT THE FRONTLOCK AS IT SYMBOLIZED MAN'S CAPACITY FOR CONTINUAL GROWTH.

IN A YEAR'S TIME, THE COMMUNITARIANS HAD LIVED IN AND MOVED FROM OVER THIRTY COMMUNITIES. FINALLY, THEY MADE THEIR WAY TO CALIFORNIA, SINGING AS THEY WENT, "YOU'LL BE SORRY YOU PULLED MY FRONTLOCK WHEN I LIVE IN HEAVEN WITH GOD." IN EARLY 1856, THEY SET THEMSELVES UP IN A FORTRESS ON A CLIFF NEAR A DESERT AND CHANGED THEIR NAME TO THE HERMITS OF CHRIST.

THOUGH THE HERMITS CUT THEIR FRONTLOCKS TO SHOW THEY NOW FELT MAN HAD LIMITED CAPACITY FOR GROWTH, IN ALL OTHER WAYS, THE HERMITS OF CHRIST WORSHIPPED IN THE TWENTIETH CENTURY MUCH AS THEY ALWAYS HAD. EACH MONK WAS STILL REQUIRED TO SLEEP WITH HIS HEAD OFF HIS BED TO REMIND HIM THAT GOD NEVER RESTS. EACH MONK MUST PUT DIRT ALL OVER HIS FOOD TO REMIND HIM "WHENCE ALL FOOD COMES, WHENCE ALL LIFE." AND STILL, EVERY OCTOBER 13, DURING HARVEST SEASON, NO ONE IS ALLOWED TO SWALLOW FOR TWENTY-FOUR HOURS, TO REMIND EACH MONK THAT EVEN THOUGH HE HAS GIVEN UP ALL WORLDLY LUXURIES, HIS BODY STILL HAS LUXURIES HE SHOULD NOT TAKE FOR GRANTED.

THE HERMITS HAVE MAINTAINED THEIR POPULATION BY LURING PASSERSBY WITH THE SIGN OUTSIDE THEIR WALLS, PEACE LIES BEYOND THIS GATE. IT WAS HERE THAT FRIAR CURRIE WAS LEFT IN A BASKET WHEN HE WAS ONLY TWO WEEKS OLD. THE HERMITS TOOK HIM IN AND HE LIVED A HAPPY AND DEVOUT LIFE. BUT AS HE GREW OLDER, HE BEGAN TO QUESTION HIS PURPOSE ON EARTH, ESPECIALLY

AFTER HE READ *THE CREED OF THE COMMUNITARIANS* BY FLANN WASHBURN.

FRIAR CURRIE'S DOUBTS DEEPENED WHEN ROYCE FRAZIER ENTERED THE MONASTERY. FRAZIER TOLD CURRIE HE WAS DISCOURAGED BY THE WORLD. DURING HIS FIFTEEN YEARS OF SOCIAL WORK IN WEST LOS ANGELES, FRAZIER HAD SEEN VIOLENCE, INCEST, DISEASE, STARVATION, RACISM—HE HAD EVEN SEEN A MOTHER SELL HER BABY FOR DRUG MONEY. FRIAR CURRIE WAS SHOCKED TO LEARN THAT SUCH A WORLD EXISTED. (WHILE NOT FORBIDDEN, TALK OF THE OUTSIDE WORLD WAS DISCOURAGED BY HERMIT ELDERS, WHO ENCOURAGED THE FRIARS TO CONCENTRATE ON WORSHIP.)

"IS NO ONE DOING ANYTHING ABOUT THIS?" FRIAR CURRIE ASKED FRAZIER.

"THERE ARE NOT ENOUGH PEOPLE TO HELP," FRAZIER ANSWERED.

CURRIE WAS DEEPLY SADDENED BY WHAT HE HAD LEARNED. HE BEGAN HAVING TROUBLE SLEEPING. HE COULDN'T EAT. FINALLY HE SPOKE TO THE FATHER ABBOT. CURRIE TOLD HIM OF HIS DISCUSSIONS WITH FRIAR FRAZIER. CURRIE SAID HE THOUGHT IT WAS WRONG FOR THE FRIARS TO STAY INSIDE THE WALLS OF A MONASTERY WHILE THE OUTSIDE WORLD WAS SO DEPRAVED. INSTEAD THEY SHOULD GO OUT AND TRY TO HELP AS MANY PEOPLE AS POSSIBLE BY TEACHING THEM THE WORD OF GOD. "IF WE COULD PERSUADE PEOPLE TO LEAD VIRTUOUS LIVES BY TEACHING THEM THE WORD OF THE LORD, WE WOULD PROVIDE THEM SOLACE IN THIS WORLD AND ENSURING THEIR ETERNAL HAPPINESS IN THE NEXT," HE SAID. "IS THAT NOT OUR PURPOSE?"

THE ABBOT TOLD CURRIE THAT WORLDLY SERVICE WAS NOT THE CALLING OF THE HERMITS. IF, HOWEVER, FRIAR CURRIE SINCERELY WISHED TO HELP MANKIND, FATHER ABBOT SAID HE WOULD NOT STAND IN HIS WAY. "BUT," HE SAID, "YOU'RE ASKING FOR IT."

FRIAR CURRIE WOULD NOT BE INTERVIEWED FOR THIS BOOK, BUT HE MADE HIS JOURNALS AVAILABLE TO US.

October 2, 1982

And there was morning and there was evening and that is the end of my first week in the outside world.

And I have been discouraged many times in the week. I am working hard but my work seems futile. Every day I talk to people at the Tomlinson Center for Unwed Mothers, the Hamblin Drug and Alcohol Rehabilitation Clinic, the Rainbow House for Runaways. At night I stand under the LeToya Avenue underpass and talk to the men and women who socialize and sell things there. When I think of how many people there are in the world, the number I am able to reach is very small.

Now tonight I saw a mother and a daughter and the mother was beating the daughter with a stick. And I came between the mother and her child and I said unto the mother that by beating her child she was denying herself a place in God's blessed kingdom. I told her to drop the stick. She did. And she begged for help and I took her to the Hamblin Drug and Alcohol Rehabilitation Center. And when we came to Hamblin's she asked if there was a Bible she could have. And I was overjoyed. I had finally helped someone. But it has been seven days and I have talked to sixty-eight people and I have only reached one. Sixty-eight attempts, one success. This could take forever.

And I know nothing of the ways of the world and must rely upon the learnedness of others. And God knows this and in His goodness He has brought me a man of infinite knowledge, a man who calls himself Mr. Bucky Schwerdloff. Now Mr. Bucky Schwerdloff was sitting next to me in the Adios Amigos Mexican

food restaurant and he told me about the "movie studio" that belonged to his father. A movie is a miracle.
It is a photograph that moves and talks. It is like a star
because you can see it in the dark.

Bucky said millions of people will see one movie.
And I said this would be a powerful way to spread a
message. And he said it was. And I thought this was the
way for me.

And I asked Bucky where I could make a movie.
And he said, "You'll have to start at the bottom somewhere and work your way up." I asked him if there was
work I could do at the bottom of his studio. He told me
they were poor. Now I am overjoyed. Tomorrow I will
begin begging for the Mr. Schwerdloff Studio.

Currie—Friar Currie—had been listening to me and Reed and he was full of questions about the movies. He'd never seen one. I couldn't believe they didn't have a Movie Night at his monastery—we always did at camp. It's no wonder he left. So I told him about the studio. The more I talked about Dad and how he'd built a small rug factory into the greatest movie studio in the world, the more I realized I *had* to keep it open—for Dad and the girls. The girls had said it would be a happy day when the studio was finally out of our lives, but they didn't fool me. They had to care about it: it was our last link with Dad.

Okay, so I decided to keep the studio open. And right away I started getting ideas. Like it occurred to me that none of the other studios had a monk on the payroll and that Friar Currie's working for us would influence God when He decided which movie studios had popular movies and which did not. I remembered that old saying, "God helps those who go to church."

The first person I told I was keeping the studio open was Reed Rayman, and he was really happy because he said the thing he wanted most in the whole world was for the studio to stay open. I said I was glad he felt that way because it was important for everyone on the team to believe in what we were doing, and I was sorry but I would have to fire him.

I said, "Keeping the studio open isn't enough. I want it to be a place that will make my sisters and my late father and, yes, me proud again. I can see I'm going to have to run it myself."

If I was going to keep the studio open, we had to do something different than what we had been doing. Our policy had been to make several pictures and hope that one of them would be a blockbuster and pay for the rest. This was stupid. Why not just make the blockbuster? That's what a restaurant does. Take McDonald's. They serve just hamburgers, no liver. Where other restaurants are losing money on their liver and letting hamburgers pull the boat, at McDonald's, hamburgers *are* the boat. Because of this, McDonald's is a very successful hamburger store. So I used that as my model. Some people thought I was wrong. They said, "Aren't you putting all your eggs in one basket?" Of course I was. That was my strategy. Some people said, "But then you don't have anything to fall back on." I didn't want to tell them, but you don't want to fall back on eggs.

So, I needed a blockbuster. I'd seen an article that said there were only two directors who turned out one blockbuster after another—Steven Spielberg and Ferris Keneally. I decided to get one of them to do a picture for us. If I couldn't get them, I wouldn't keep the studio open. Oh, and I also decided to try to get Sylvester Stallone. Stallone wasn't as commercial as the others but I was willing to take the risk for an artist like him.

One of the reasons I wanted to make a success of the studio was that it would mean some extra money for my sisters. Whenever I talked with them, they were always pinched for money. I don't think they were savers.

I decided not to tell them about my plans to take over the studio until it was definite.

CHAPTER 4

PAN LEFT, PAN RIGHT:
THE SEARCH FOR A DIRECTOR

FROM BUCKY SCHWERDLOFF'S "NOTES TO MYSELF" PAD

October 5, 1982

1. Directors. Try again to reach Ferris Keneally. If does
   not call back by noon, set up appointment with
   Spielberg. Must move ahead.

FROM FRIAR CURRIE'S JOURNAL

October 7, 1982

And my days have been glad ones. When I told Bucky
that I was here to help the needy, he drove me to
Dave's, a private psychiatric clinic in Beverly Hills.
Now I go every morning to Dave's and talk to the
patients. I have made friends with a man who can
make beautiful bubbles from his saliva. Each one has a
rainbow in it.

After Dave's, Bucky and I went up out of the studio in his car to the Universal City so that Bucky could meet Mr. Steven Spielberg. While Bucky was in his meeting I took the Universal City Tour. When I was getting out of the car to take the tour, part of my robe became ensnared in the door of the car. Now my robe was riven up to my waist. And this is a great hardship as it is my only robe. I would have waited in the car but I hoped the Universal City would be man's attempt to create the City of God which St. Augustine wrote about so beautifully and certainly I wanted to see that. I held the riven parts together.

On the tour, we went into the dressing room of Miss Angela Lansbury. Miss Angela Lansbury was not there but her garments were. And she had an exceedingly nice robe that was green and long like mine but it was not ripped like mine. And I coveted it and asked to buy it. Now there was great laughter and I was red with shame and I hastened back to the car.

I turned on the radio and tried to find some hymns but I could not find any. Then I listened to KPTT, "your place to be for country music." The first person to sing was Miss Patsy Cline. She sang, "I Fall to Pieces." After tearing my robe, I knew how she felt.

I got out of the car and prayed to God to help Miss Patsy Cline. Then she sang, "I Love You So Much It Hurts." And I felt better.

Mr. Spielberg told Bucky that he cannot labor for the Mr. Schwerdloff Studio. But Bucky is not disheartened. He is full of plans for the studio.

I have a plan too. I told Bucky we should make a movie of the beautiful portrait we have at the monastery of Flann Washburn. Bucky laughed heartily. Then he said I had a lot to learn about the movies.

With Bucky as my teacher, I will learn quickly.

October 10, 1982

1. Think of things to do if I keep the studio open.

2. Here's a great idea for a movie: Through some kind of freaky accident, I don't know what yet, maybe something to do with a microwave, the parents of a large family start to get one year younger every day. Lots of laughs as they get younger than their own kids: their oldest son grounds them when he finds out they were drinking at a cocktail party; truant officer can make them quit their jobs and go to school . . . Good Line: "But I already had braces!" Good title: *Countdown*. Think this could be *very* big. Hot dog!

3. Call Julia at 1:30 her time. She should be out to lunch. Tell secretary to tell Julia to call back. Then, duck call so Julia doesn't find out I didn't close the studio. (If Julia answers, *hang up*.)

4. Meet Sylvester Stallone at 1:00 at Spago. Some thoughts on this:

    1. Be your own man. Don't order what he orders, unless it sounds really good.

    2. Don't tell Sylvester Stallone great idea for movie (*Countdown*), but tell him you have a great idea. (Maybe tell him a little, if you want, but not the great part. Otherwise, he could steal.)

5. Find out what time my time 1:30 Julia's time is.

October 9, 1982

. . . I have been thinking about my movie of the Flann Washburn painting. I have thought of a way to give it more action. In the beginning the movie could be only of the canvas but then, toward the end, I could frame it.

At Dave's I told this idea to the man who blows bubbles with his saliva. And though he thinks this is a good idea, he says it is a bad idea because it is too good an idea for the movies. "You are good," he said, "and movies are bad. Stay away from movies."

I do not see how movies can be bad if they reach so many people.

Stallone said the film he really wanted to do was a biography of Edgar Allan Poe. First of all, I didn't tell him this, but a biography's a book. Second, as it turned out, he didn't even know who Edgar Allan Poe was! Stallone thought Poe was a writer!

When I told him, you know, that Poe was the father of Poland, he could not admit that he was wrong. It was sad. To think that this was the same man who had written the *Rocky* pictures!

So I told him, as gently as I could, that I couldn't work with him and he said he wouldn't work with me for all the money in China. Of course, they don't even have money in China, they use sticks or something, but I knew what he meant. It didn't bother me. He was just embarrassed for not knowing who Edgar Allan Poe was.

When I left the restaurant, I felt great, really great. Two of the three directors that I felt could save the studio were no longer available. Only Keneally was left. Good omen, I thought. He was my first choice.

FROM FRIAR CURRIE'S JOURNAL

October 13, 1982

And now it has been three days and still Bucky has not met with Mr. Keneally. Bucky made a telephone call to the agent of Mr. Keneally and the agent said that Mr. Keneally was not available. And Bucky was "red hot" and concocted a plot. Tomorrow he will telephone the agent and he will say that he is Mr. Keneally's physician and that he has now noticed something on an old X-ray that he had thought was a shadow but now thinks is something else. And Bucky will ask for a telephone number where he can reach Mr. Keneally.

I admonished Bucky, for to lie is to sin. He said he was going to do it nevertheless, so I prayed to God for his forgiveness.

Then Bucky bought me an Eskimo Pie and let me steer the car from Beech Street to the studio. And I felt broad delight.

11:20 P.M.

I hope I am not being corrupted. I must remember: Eskimo Pies and steering are not why I left the Hermits.

JULIA SCHWERDLOFF BUSH

I was getting worried.

Bucky had been in California for several days and I hadn't spoken to him; I kept missing his calls. I hadn't seen anything in the papers about the studio closing and I wondered if he'd lost his nerve, or if . . . I don't know. *Something* was wrong. Then that postcard came and I knew.

BUCKY'S POSTCARD

Dear Julia,

Has become impossible to call. No phones working in state due to break-up of AT&T. All lines
down, everything a big mess. But don't worry.
Everything is great.

Lots of love,

Bucky

BUCKY SCHWERDLOFF

For a while there, it looked like we'd reached a dead end with Ferris. I'd call his home, no answer. I wrote him care of a woman I'd been told he lived with but the letter was returned, marked "Addressee off his rocker." I talked to his parents—I guess they're not too close to him; they said he'd been dead for twenty-three years—I spoke to the Directors Guild, and a lady who knew him at AA.

I just couldn't find him. Finally, I told my secretary to get everyone together because I wanted to tell them that I was closing the studio down. If I couldn't start off with a great picture and a great director, I didn't want to bother. And the banks weren't going to fool around either with just any little movie. We needed a blockbuster.

Before I talked to everyone, I sat in Dad's old office. I felt so guilty, but I didn't know what else I could do. I was walking out the door when the phone rang. It was Friar Currie. He was calling from the mental home with good news.

He said, "I have seen Keneally."
I said, "Hot dog!"

FROM FRIAR CURRIE'S JOURNAL

October 24, 1982

It has happened that the man at Dave's who blows bubbles from his saliva is Ferris Keneally, the director Bucky so desires to have labor for him. Hot dog!

I telephoned Bucky that I had found him. And Bucky made a joyful noise.

"Tell him we would like him to make a movie for us," Bucky said.

And I know just what movie to tell him he should make.

BUCKY SCHWERDLOFF

At first, Ferris didn't think he could make a blockbuster. I think having a nervous breakdown really undermined his confidence. But I'm pretty good with people, I think, and he finally said yes.

I was so happy. Keneally was the biggest director in Hollywood. When I told everyone at the studio that I was keeping the studio open and that our first film would be directed by Ferris Keneally, they clapped really loud. A lot of them came up to me after the speech to thank me and shake my hand. Some had tears in their eyes.

The real thrill of the day, though, was walking back into Dad's old office, an office I would now make my own, and calling my sisters to give them the great news.

Bucky reached me at the bank. I was in a meeting with the economic minister from Argentina. Bucky said he had wonderful news. He sounded so excited I thought, *He's getting married.* But then he said it. He said, "I'm taking over the studio."

I said, "But, Bucky, you don't know anything about the movie business."

He said, "Don't worry—I've hired a monk! Plus, we've got the hottest director in Hollywood—if we can get him out of the mental home!"

I couldn't even . . . my breath just went out of me. My annual share of sheltering Bucky from the truth about himself was running at $55,000 a year. I didn't want to let him down, but I couldn't afford for him to have another triumph in business. And, I know it's awful, but when I heard him say he was taking on a third business, I dropped the phone and had to lie down on the floor. It was so cool there and, for a second, I felt better.

AMELIA SCHWERDLOFF DUFFEE

It was the perfect business for him. It was already losing $100 million a year.

BUCKY SCHWERDLOFF

After I called the girls, I sat by myself in Dad's office, my feet on his desk, with a glass of champagne. I looked out the window. Huge black clouds came out of nowhere and it started to rain like I'd never seen it. A giant bolt of lightning ripped across the sky. Then there was another one, even bigger. It hit a tree and knocked it over. The tree nearly smashed into the studio.

Good omen! I thought. Rain makes things grow.

CHAPTER 5

CLOSE-UP: FERRIS KENEALLY

BRYANT WOODS, vice-president of production, MGM/UA

I don't want to sound cute but it was just like an old movie: one of the great old studios is about to go under, then the greatest director in Hollywood says he'll do a movie for them. He has never directed a failure and, finally, after all those years, the studio has a chance to succeed again and all Hollywood is rooting for them.

That's how we were when we heard that Keneally was doing a movie for Schwerdloff. Everyone watched and held their breath and crossed their fingers and rooted for them to fail.

At Dave's I had been thinking very seriously about my life. I was forty-three years old and I hadn't done a single thing I was proud of. That made me sad. I knew I could never retrieve the years I had lost, so I vowed to use the rest of my life as if each new day was a chance to make up for the waste of days gone by.

But I didn't know how to do that. What means? Then Bucky called and asked if I would direct a picture for them. I had thought I would not go back to movies as I blamed the medium for my unhappiness. But it was I—it was my misuse of the medium that had made me so unhappy. The friar made me see that. He said, "Can you not use movies to enrich life?"

I said, "Somebody could, but not me, evidently."

He said, "Why can't you?"

And, you know what? I had no answer. Why couldn't I make a film that would enrich our understanding of each other? I mean, look, look here: just because I had made only big commercial vulgar films didn't mean I wasn't capable of making a profound film. I simply had to pick more profound material. So I began thinking about making a small, personal film—an art film for an independent company, some highbrow operation that wouldn't care about money. I saw it as a way to fuse my intellectual and emotional aspirations with my technical abilities. For the first time, I felt as if I were on the right track.

So when Bucky called, I automatically said, "No," because a studio film was exactly what I didn't want to do. Bucky said, "You don't have to make a studio film—shoot it outside." This softened me up. At least he has a sense of humor.

Still, I said, "No," and he said I could do any movie I wanted. I said, "Any movie? Even a small, heartfelt artsy film?"

He said, "Sure, as long as it's a blockbuster."

I said, "Oh, no, I can't make a blockbuster for you."

He said, "Any movie you make would be a block-buster."

I said, "Why thank you, old sport." I must say I was touched by his faith.

DR. YALE ZIMET, Ferris Keneally's psychiatrist and chief of staff at Dave's

Frankly, I was quite against Ferris's release. Foremost, I felt he wasn't stable enough and that a premature release would jeopardize his mental health for the rest of his life. Also, we always, well, to tell you the truth, after all of us have evaluated a new patient, we make kind of a . . . well, frankly, we take bets. We bet on how long the patient will be here, if he'll get better or worse—you know, just little things to keep the job interesting. And I had bet that Ferris would be here for eighteen to twenty-four months—our choices come in six-month intervals—but he'd only been here eight months when he decided to leave. That meant Dr. Simons was going to win. He always cleans up, that Simons. He really understands the mentally ill. Some people have it, I guess; some don't.

I told Bucky that Ferris was not ready to work. He was at a very delicate stage in his treatment and to remove him now and thrust him into the world was like . . . well, have you ever had a cake in the oven and after, say, fifteen minutes or so, just as it's beginning to form, to stand up a little on its own and be like other cakes, you take it out and you cut it and it quivers and collapses and is no use as a cake? No, of course you haven't. No one has. It would be stupid. It wouldn't help you. It wouldn't help the cake. That's what I told Bucky. I pleaded with him. I said, "Ferris can't solve his problems yet. *Please!* Don't take him out of the oven yet! Not till he's done!"

But Bucky said, "Yale, I've got to disagree with you.

When my sister Julia and I were little, we were going to bake a cake but we never did because we ate all the batter first. That's the best part!" To tell you the truth, after meeting him, I thought Bucky ought to check in here himself.

I tried my best to keep Ferris at Dave's, but there was nothing I could legally do. He wasn't dangerous. But whatever is next to dangerous, he was that. This is not to say he wasn't a thoroughly charming fellow—he had great force of personality. I remember the night he persuaded me, against my professional instincts, to go through the clinic and short-sheet certain of the patients' beds. Short-sheeting beds in a psychiatric ward was irresponsible of Ferris but we viewed it as a forward step because it showed he was not hampered by what other people thought of him.

FELICIA KENEALLY, mother of Ferris Keneally

Two years before we had Ferris, we'd had another child—Brian. We loved Brian very much but we felt we could do better. So, we had Ferris, who, from the word go, was as smart as a whip. Even the nurses said they'd never seen a baby so smart. When I brought him home from the hospital, he signed us out. The nurses made quite a fuss about that but, to be honest, I was embarrassed. He spelled our name with two *n*s and one *l*. A lot of people make that mistake, but, still, your own son!

Ferris had so much potential, we knew he was the child we would lavish our attentions on. We realized Brian would have to go. So it was off to the A & P with little Brian, all dolled up in his Sunday best. I remember it was a hot summer day so we left him in Produce. We thought he'd be more comfortable there—they have a lot of ice and they're always watering things down. He really did look cute as a button on top of that bib lettuce—we almost wanted to keep him.

Welp! that was the last we saw of little Brian. We assume some customer picked him up and gave him a nice home. Of course, I'll never know—I don't shop there anymore. It's really not a very clean store and it had the most awful odor.

Ferris was a very smart baby. When he was two, for our anniversary, he built us a compound/complex sentence with a beautiful series of gerund phrases. We still have it.

At three, Ferris started writing a novel, but around three and a half, he got blocked and put it aside. He thought it was shallow.

Really, looking back, that was the beginning of the end.

FRITZ KENEALLY, father of Ferris Keneally

Frankly, Ferris was a huge disappointment to my wife and myself. The school kept saying he was a genius, but I sure never saw it. He never finished that novel. That really bugs me. I don't care if you're three and a half or if you're thirty, you should finish what you start.

A lot of people think Ferris was a genius for going to Harvard when he was only fifteen. Big deal. What was he supposed to do after he graduated from high school?

I don't know. . . . Sometimes I think it was a mistake that Brian was the one we took to the A & P.

HAROLD ENGLISH, college roommate of Ferris Keneally

Ferris was the smartest person I knew at Harvard. Freshman year, all he did was work. We were in this pretty wild dorm and there were always parties. One night I persuaded him to put down his books and come out and have a beer. At that time, Ferris was something of an oddity—the youngest student at Harvard, very shy—but after that night, he really relaxed.

Junior year, Ferris fell in love with Donna Zeng, but she wouldn't give him the time of day. She was having this hot affair with Yasir Sharif and they spent every waking minute in bed together. But Ferris wouldn't give up. All through the fall and winter he tried to win her over. He'd send her things, he'd write her poems. I asked him why he wanted Donna so much. He said, "She's my idea of the perfect woman. She reminds me so little of my mother."

That spring, Donna was in terrible academic shape. It looked like she might flunk out. Suddenly, right before exams, she developed this deep love for Ferris. They started going out. He primed her for her exams. He helped her write her papers. Then she asked him to write her Moral Philosophy take-home final because, she said, she had to plant a tree for Israel that night. Ferris wrote the final.

Donna said she would pick the exam up the next morning but Ferris took it by her room that night. When he went in, he found her in bed with Yasir. Ferris was hysterical. For three days, he was like a maniac. Then

73

suddenly—it was weird—he became calm. We figured he'd worked it out.

The next day in the *Crimson**, there was a full page ad he'd taken out. There was a picture of Donna and, underneath it, it said, "This is DONNA ZENG. In Chinese, ZENG means DOG VOMIT. Four days ago, while I was taking Donna Dog Vomit's Moral Philosophy take-home final, she was spreading her legs for this maggot." And there was a picture of Yasir. "Her final is a dishonest piece of shit and so is she."

We had a friend that worked at the *Crimson;* he got the ad in for Ferris. The *Crimson* got in a lot of trouble for that. The next day they had to run a retraction: "Though it is true that Donna Zeng spread her legs for the maggot pictured in this paper yesterday, it has been brought to our attention that Zeng in Chinese does not mean 'dog vomit.' The *Crimson* regrets any embarrassment this error might have caused Miss Zeng."

*Harvard's undergraduate newspaper.

FELICIA KENEALLY

Ferris was the youngest student at Harvard but he wasn't the youngest student ever at Harvard and, naturally, we were disappointed about that. He said he would make it up to us and he did: he graduated early, at the end of his junior year*. Ferris's work was of such a high caliber, the faculty voted the night before graduation to let Ferris graduate early. He said the dean himself had told him, "You can go no further here." Anyway, it all happened so quickly, Ferris didn't have time to notify us. He tried but he said our line was busy.

Then Ferris was a Rhodes scholar**. He met a lovely English girl while he was there and later they both taught at Oxford***. Ferris and the girl were engaged but he lost her at Versailles, in the Hall of Mirrors, and never found her again. He was very upset and he took a long, contemplative cruise.****

*In fact, Keneally was expelled over the Donna Zeng incident.
**In fact, according to Keneally, he was drunk for a year in Nantucket.
***In fact, Keneally fell in love with Debby Duncan, a palm reader from Marblehead, Massachusetts. When Duncan saw infidelity in their future, Keneally, to prove his love, stole a plane and flew them to Juárez, Mexico, for a romantic weekend. Keneally was shocked when he came out of the shower and found Duncan in bed with a bellhop. In a rage, Keneally assaulted the couple with his suitcase, and it was one of those old, hard ones. Keneally was arrested and jailed.
****In fact, Keneally escaped from jail and lived by stealing from churches in Texas and the Southwest.

When he got back . . . well, it wasn't simply that he wasn't a genius, it was as if he no longer had any interest in *being* a genius. That was when he told us he had decided to go into the movies. When he said that, I looked at him and thought, *Welp! You're not worth thinking about anymore.*

Fritz and I talked it over and agreed that Ferris had had more than enough time to make us proud and he had failed. So we divided up the phone book and called all our friends and told them that Ferris was dead.

FRITZ KENEALLY

After we decided that Ferris had died, I was thinking of the assorted ways he'd disappointed us, but I did think there was one thing he'd done that made me proud. He graduated early from Harvard. I don't care what his mother says, that was quite an achievement, and when I was on the phone with him, explaining that we could not send him his skis because he was dead, I told him so.

. . .

IN 1959, KENEALLY MOVED TO LOS ANGELES IN THE HOPES OF GET-
TING INTO THE MOVIE BUSINESS. HE TRIED FOR SEVERAL MONTHS TO
FIND WORK BUT NO ONE WOULD SEE HIM. KENEALLY DECIDED HE
WOULD TRY TO GET AN INTERVIEW WITH AN EXECUTIVE OUTSIDE
ONE OF THE STUDIOS.

AT THE TIME, JUSTIN STONE WAS ONE OF THE MOST POWERFUL
EXECUTIVES IN HOLLYWOOD. HE WAS ALSO KNOWN AS A GREAT
PATRON OF THE ANIMALS; HIS NICKNAME WAS DR. DOOLITTLE.*

ONE MORNING, KENEALLY FOLLOWED STONE AS HE WAS DRIV-
ING TO WORK. AS STONE APPROACHED THE STUDIO, KENEALLY
PULLED UP BESIDE HIM AND THEN CRASHED INTO HIS CAR. STONE
GOT OUT OF THE CAR SCREAMING BUT KENEALLY EXPLAINED THAT

---

*In the late 1950s, killing squirrels was the latest fad among Califor-
nia teenagers. It was Stone who organized the statewide campaign
that resulted in criminal penalties for the killing of squirrels except
in self-defense.

HE HAD SWERVED TO AVOID A SQUIRREL. THE REASON HE WAS SPEEDING, KENEALLY TOLD STONE, WAS THAT HE WAS DUE AT THE DOG HOSPITAL WHERE HE DID VOLUNTEER WORK, PETTING THE ANIMALS BEFORE THEIR OPERATIONS. FURTHERMORE, IT WOULD BE SOME TIME BEFORE KENEALLY COULD PAY FOR THE DAMAGE HE HAD DONE TO STONE'S CAR BECAUSE HE HAD ONLY RECENTLY MOVED TO CALIFORNIA AND HAD NO JOB YET.

STONE APOLOGIZED FOR SCREAMING AND TOLD KENEALLY THAT IF HE WAS AT ALL INTERESTED IN WORKING IN THE MOVIES HE SHOULD STOP BY STONE'S OFFICE ON HIS WAY BACK FROM THE HOSPITAL. KENEALLY SAID HE'D NEVER THOUGHT ABOUT THE MOVIES BUT MIGHT STOP BY.

WITHIN A YEAR, KENEALLY WAS DIRECTING A MOVIE FOR STONE AT 20TH CENTURY-FOX. HE HAD STEPPED IN TO REPLACE RICHARD LESTER ON *5, 6, 7, 8!* AND DURING THE NEXT TWENTY-FOUR YEARS HE DIRECTED SEVENTEEN FILMS, ALL OF WHICH WERE ENORMOUSLY POPULAR. OF *VARIETY*'S TOP TEN ALL-TIME GROSSING FILMS, SEVEN WERE DIRECTED BY KENEALLY. THEY INCLUDE:

1. *5, 6, 7, 8!* (1960), STARRING THE BRITISH ROCK GROUP 1, 2, 3, 4! THIS WAS THE FIRST 1, 2, 3, 4 FILM AND IT WAS THE ONE WHERE 2 AND 3 FALL IN LOVE WITH THE SAME GIRL, WHO HAD BEEN HIRED BY THEIR MANAGER TO KEEP THEM FROM FALLING IN LOVE. THIS FILM INSPIRED THE UNBUCKLED-BELT LOOK AND INTRODUCED THE SONG, "YES, NO, OH, ALL RIGHT."

2. *ON YOUR MARKS, GET SET, GO!* (1962), KENEALLY'S TURN-OF-THE-CENTURY CROSS-COUNTRY RACE MOVIE WITH OVER THIRTY-THREE STARS AND CAMEOS. CONTESTANTS HAD TO GET FROM BOSTON TO SAN FRANCISCO AND COULD NOT GO BY CAR, TRAIN, PLANE, OR BOAT. THIS WAS THE FILM THAT HAD BUDDY HACKETT ON STILTS FALLING IN LOVE WITH ETHEL MERMAN ON A POGO STICK. THROUGHOUT THE MOVIE, THE AUDIENCE IS RETURNED TO THE STARTING GATE WHERE JIMMY DURANTE, ON SKATES, KEEPS FALLING DOWN AND

SAYING FUNNY THINGS ("HERE TODAY, HERE TOMORROW!" ETC.)

3. *WHERE'S WHITEY?* (1964), THE MERRY ROMP ABOUT WHITEY THE BUNNY WHO JUMPS INTO THE ENGINE OF A ROCKET HEADED FOR THE MOON. THE ROCKET GOES HAYWIRE AND, INSTEAD OF LANDING ON THE MOON, LANDS IN SCOTLAND. THE ASTRONAUTS, JACK LEMMON AND TONY CURTIS, THINK THEY'RE ON THE MOON. WHEN MEN IN KILTS WALK BY, TONY CURTIS WHISPERS, "IF THIS IS WHAT THE WOMEN HERE LOOK LIKE, I DON'T WANT TO MEET THE MEN!" CLAIRE PECK, WHO WOULD MARRY KENEALLY DURING THE FILMING, PLAYED THE SCOTTISH LASS WHO HID THE ASTRONAUTS IN HER FATHER'S HEDGEROWS.

4. *SSSSH, SSSSH, BOOM!* (1969), KENEALLY'S BOMB-IN-THE-LIBRARY-OF-CONGRESS MOVIE, STARRING OMAR SHARIF, RICHARD WIDMARK, AND TIPPI HEDREN. ITS MOST FAMOUS SCENE WAS SHOT INSIDE A TRAY IN THE CARD CATALOG WHILE TIPPI HEDREN FLIPS FRANTICALLY THROUGH THE CARDS IN A DESPERATE ATTEMPT TO LOCATE THE ONE BOOK THAT HAS THE FORMULA FOR DEFUSING THE BOMB. A SPECIAL CARD CATALOG CAMERA HAD TO BE BUILT.

5. *THE RE-ESCAPERS* (1971), WHICH STARRED FRANK SINATRA, LEE MARVIN, AND YUL BRYNNER AS THREE PRISONERS WHO TUNNEL OUT OF A GERMAN PRISON ONLY TO DISCOVER THEY HAVE TUNNELED INTO A CONCENTRATION CAMP. JOINING UP THERE WITH CHARLES BRONSON AND RAQUEL WELCH, THEY RE-ESCAPE. [KENEALLY DID NOT DIRECT THE INFERIOR SEQUEL *THE RE-RE-ESCAPERS*.]

6. *SWOOPER* (1978), STARRING ROBERT REDFORD AS BOTANIST/ADVENTURER DASH SWOOPER WHO TRAVELS TO AFRICA IN SEARCH OF A BUTTERFLY WHOSE ANTENNAE CONTAIN CODES FOR GERMAN WAR SECRETS. THE SCENE MOST PEOPLE REMEMBER IS THE ONE WHERE SWOOPER, TEMPORARILY BLINDED AND CRIPPLED BY POISON DARTS, OUTRUNS AN AVALANCHE.

7. *THE BLINKIES* (1982), ABOUT THE EVERYDAY STRUGGLES OF A FAMILY OF EXTRATERRESTRIALS WHO MOVE NEXT DOOR TO A FIRE DEPARTMENT IN A LONG ISLAND SUBURB. DOLLY PARTON'S THEME FROM *THE BLINKIES*, " 'XX7PQ' MEANS 'I LOVE YOU' " WON THE OSCAR FOR BEST SONG.

DR. YALE ZIMET

Though Ferris was an immensely successful man in a professional capacity, he was very unhappy personally. His self-esteem was psychotically low. Why? I think his parents' decision to kill him had an impact. This has led Ferris to seek love from everyone he meets—studio executives, cabdrivers, senators, criminals. This obsession with being loved also explains his choice of films. Ferris always directed films with the widest appeal.

Ferris initially came to me after his first movie opened. He was feeling empty and depressed and couldn't figure out why.

We looked at his life. He seemed to be having a problem forming a lasting, loving relationship with a woman. He estimated that in the past year, he had gone out with a hundred women. He was so afraid of a repeat of the incident with Donna Zeng—namely that his lover would have an affair behind his back—that he never went out with a woman long enough for a relationship to develop.

And yet, as I say, Ferris desperately wanted love. To get love, of course, one must be willing to give love and Ferris was in no position for that. He was clamped shut like an oyster. I told him he must stick the fork in himself and open himself up— show his pearl to others. It took a long time for Ferris to accept this. It wasn't really until Claire that he fully shucked himself.

CLAIRE PECK, actress and ex-wife of Ferris Keneally

Fer and I met in the sixties. I was in L.A. working with Intertwine, a theater company. We were doing *The Electric Raspberry,* a rock version of *King Henry IV, Part II.* I was playing Duke of Somerset. Intertwine always cast only women in Shakespeare plays to protest the Elizabethan practice of casting only men.

Fer came back after the show one night and asked me out for a drink. I suggested we go to this bistro I knew for cappuccino. Fer loved the idea. In those days no one went out for cappuccino. They went out for coffee and cream.

Then he offered me a part in that rabbit movie, the *Whitey* movie. I didn't want to take it—I wanted to do serious roles—but my acting coach Drago said, "If you want to climb the tree, you have to step in the dirt." So I accepted the part because of that and also because I couldn't bear to be away from Fer. While we were shooting, he asked me to marry him and I said yes.

Our marriage was beautiful at the beginning, rewarding, a real union! We talked about our shared love for literature and drama and how when Fer was through with the *Whitey* movie, we would do a serious film together, a real film, not another rabbit film. But then he did *Time Bus.* While technically this was not another rabbit film, it wasn't the serious film we dreamed about. In the film we conceived, I would play a social worker named Dusty. The film would be about my frustrations and dilemmas on the job and how I fall in love with one of my clients, a retarded man named Earl. The film was to be called, *One and One Is Three*.

Then I became pregnant with Somerset. It was a natural childbirth. This was years before anyone else did natural. Fer was in the room with me and he was a wonderful partner. I had planned to go back to work right away but I loved being with Somerset so much, I didn't feel in any hurry. I was happy to wait for the *One and One* screenplay that Fer was writing for me. Those were happy days for a while. Fer and I'd get up together and give Somerset her bath, then Somerset and I would play and Fer would work on the screenplay. After a couple of weeks, though, Fer began having doubts about the screenplay. He wouldn't show it to me. He became sour. He kept saying, "I don't have anything new to say." Then he said, "Maybe there isn't anything new to say." He grew despondent. Finally, he agreed to direct *Ssssh, Ssssh, Boom!* He said he was doing it because he was worried about our finances and that he would work on *One and One* when *Ssssh* was done. But as soon as he finished *Ssssh*, he went right into *The Re-Escapers*. When I asked him about *One and One*, he said it wouldn't be ready for a while but that if I wanted to be in *The Re-Escapers*, I could play Switchblade.* I said I wanted more serious work and he promised he'd finish our movie soon. But I knew by then that he wouldn't. He was afraid of it or something. It got so that he wouldn't go in that room.

While he was filming *The Re-Escapers*, I got a call from Berthold Leithauser. He offered me the part of the treacherous psychiatrist in *The Attendant*. I was thrilled. It was just the sort of part I'd trained for. And I was honored to work for Berthold. When I told Fer, he said he was very excited for me. But now, of course, I realize it must have just killed him.

*This part was eventually played by Raquel Welch.

83

This was when we began growing apart. I became a regular in Berthold's films. I received a fair share of critical acclaim, cover stories, awards. But I don't judge my work by those standards—in fact, I give my trophies and plaques and clippings to the poor—but Fer takes those things very seriously. Each award for me was an award he wasn't winning. But it wasn't the old cliché: my star rising, his fading. He was unquestionably the most successful director in Hollywood history. But this didn't bring him any peace. He became bitter and small-spirited. He started to make fun of my work. The only happiness he seemed to find was with our daughter. He could forget about everything with Somerset.

But finally, by 1974, there was nothing left to our marriage. We lived together but rarely spoke. Eventually, I divorced him and married Berthold. No one had ever married Berthold before. I was the first.

DR. YALE ZIMET

Through the seventies, despite the popularity of his work, Ferris became more and more unhappy. Although many of my colleagues do not agree with me, I often encourage my patients to run away from their problems. If you ask me, a change of scenery is as good as a change of attitude.

So, I told Ferris he should get out of Hollywood for a while. He had been preparing a new project, *The Blinkies*, with a total lack of enthusiasm. He postponed the commencement of shooting for a few weeks and went East. He was particularly excited about the trip because he had decided to go back to Harvard for his reunion. He saw the reunion as the perfect antidote to his depression. He assumed his expulsion would be forgotten or overlooked and that he would be welcomed back as one of Harvard's sons, especially in light of his outstanding achievements in the movie business. After all, he was the richest man in Hollywood. Instead, the president, in his speech, singled out Ferris's class for their remarkable level of intellectual accomplishment and praised them for their selfless decisions *not* to make money; that by sacrificing for artistic and humanitarian causes, he said, they had enriched Harvard and the world. Ferris's self-loathing grew when he sat next to a man at the reunion dinner who had sold his leg so that he could complete his slim volume of verse.

After the reunion, Ferris returned to Hollywood to

begin filming *The Blinkies*. The experience at Harvard was clearly still with him, so, as it turned out, I was completely wrong in advising him to leave town. Oh, well, you win a few, you lose a few.

GANZIE STANTON, character actor

Yep, yep, I worked on *The Blink*—yep, on *The Blink*—on *The Blinkies*. Yep. I worked on every one of Ferris's, every one of his pictures, way back to the first one, yep, *5, 6, 7, 8!* He was a happier fella then, but it didn't last, nope. He soured on himself, soured on his work, thought he wasted his life, yep.

It wasn't so bad until *The Blinkies*, nope. But then he was taking it out on people, yep. I remember, I remember on *The Blink*—on *The Blinkies*, little Sandy Duncan made him a suggestion. She was playing 3609X—that's what the Blinkies call their mothers—and she suggested that in the drugstore scene, yep, that instead of putting on the lipstick, she should eat it. Yep. You know! Heh-heh! And she said that, yep, she suggested that, Sandy did, and Ferris, he says, "That's a shitty suggestion!" That little girl nearly fell on the floor. But then he says, "But, it's a shitty movie—put it in!" Sandy didn't know if he was kidding or not but he wasn't, nope. He went right over to his chair and yelled, "Lights, camera, shit!" Yep.

Ferris's tactic in dealing with his problems had always been to avoid thinking about them. And so he carried them with him wherever he went. He was like a man who kept picking things up at the grocery store but never went home to unpack them. The result was that, after the Harvard reunion and the incident with his daughter, the bag he had been carrying so long finally broke and heavy cans fell on his foot and a bottle of apple juice broke and spilled all over everything. He could not go on. He had to clean up.

The incident with his daughter was . . . well, Ferris had come back from Harvard feeling worthless. He'd gone over to Claire and Berthold's to pick up Somerset for dinner. Somerset was not home yet so Ferris decided to wait in her room because, you know, he felt uncomfortable with Claire and Berthold, and also it gave him a chance to go through Somerset's things, which was something I always encouraged him to do. This time, however, Ferris made an upsetting discovery. He found a paper Somerset had written entitled, "Film as a Force for Progress: The Work of Berthold Leithauser." This so devastated Ferris, he did not wait to confront Somerset. He left the house immediately.

He went for a drive to calm down but unfortunately came to an intersection where Berthold Leithauser's *In a Tunnel Sad* was showing at the Little Jewel, and across the street Ferris's *Boogaloo* was at the Flick Barn Complex Eight. This was too much for Ferris.

Personally, I would have expected Ferris to have cracked up long before this, but the human mind—go figure it.

OFFICER STEVEN SWEENEY

At six-forty-six P.M. on September 9, Officer Laney and I received a call notifying us of a disturbance at the Flick Barn Complex Eight on Hollywood Boulevard. We proceeded to the location and found Mr. Keneally in Theater Five. The film in Theater Five was Mr. Keneally's *Boogaloo*. The theater manager, Mr. Eddie Maddox, had complained that the perpetrator, Mr. Keneally, was heckling the film and making animal noises.

We removed the perpetrator from the theater and into the patrol car. My partner and I agreed later that the perpetrator was very charming. Against regulations, we allowed him to sit up front with us and then take us to dinner. At dinner, he was very sad and said, "I've made a terrific mess of myself, haven't I?" and asked us to take him to Dave's. We weren't supposed to, but we did. We liked the perpetrator. On the way to Dave's, we let him use the siren.

ADMITTANCE FORM FOR FERRIS KENEALLY;
DAVE'S MENTAL REHABILITATION CLINIC

DATE: 2.

NAME: ~~Mud~~ FAS IN failure Keneally

ADDRESS: DON'T deserve ONE

OCCUPATION: ~~Ponderer~~ I Lower ~~America's~~ America's IQ

WHY ARE YOU HERE?: To Find out WHY I'm Here

HOW DID YOU HEAR ABOUT DAVE'S?: (Check one:)

( ) Friend?

( ) Radio or TV ad?

( ) Karen Black?

( ) Your doctor?

( ) Other? If so: No more OF this - I need Help.

DR. YALE ZIMET

When Ferris came to Dave's, his greatest fear was that he would bore the psychiatrists by talking about his problems.

The night of his arrival it took the nurses forever to get him to take his sleeping pills because he kept making the pills disappear from the cup and reappear behind the nurses' ears. The nurses loved it. Finally, Dr. Annexton had to be called in to administer the medication. Dr. Annexton very sternly told Ferris it was time to take the pills. Ferris asked him what time it was but Annexton couldn't find his watch. "There it is!" said Ferris. It was on Nurse Weil. Dr. Annexton and the nurses stayed up half the night watching Ferris's tricks.

I had difficulty with Ferris also. He was very uncommunicative. One day he didn't show up for our session. I went to look for him and found him at the phone. I asked him why he hadn't shown up and he said, "I've been trying to . . . it's just everything . . . it's Somerset's birthday. I've always spent her birthday with her and now . . . now, I can't even bring myself to call her. There's just so . . . it's just so . . . I'm just so . . . Help me, Yale."

That was the breakthrough in Ferris's treatment. From that point on, he discussed his life with candor and bravery. That's the thing about psychiatry that still amazes me. People tell you such personal things. I'm always thinking, *Aren't you embarrassed?*

I was terrifically low when I got to the nuthouse. I'm afraid the shrinks had their hands full with me but they stuck with me, never giving up, never turning away, especially Dr. Zimet. He helped me see that I had always done what my parents wanted and then what Hollywood wanted and then what my public wanted. We decided I should do what *I* wanted. When the friar told me I could do whatever I wanted at the Schwerdloff Studio, I began thinking seriously about returning to work.

When I met the friar, I was immediately attracted to him because he was . . . he was so peaceful. At Dave's I found the peace I had never known.

I talked with the friar for weeks about what the movie should be. He'd never seen a movie before, so his suggestions weren't always helpful. He tried for a long time to get me to make a movie of some painting he liked. I explained a movie had to have a story. The next day, he came in all charged up. He asked, "You wish a story?" I said, "Yes, old sport, I do."

He said, "I do not know whether this is possible or not, but, peradventure, is it legal to make a filmed version of a book—a visualization?" I said that it was and he smiled and pulled a small book from his robe. He said, "This is a masterpiece. And it is the most magnificent I have ever read. You should read it. It will fill up your heart with light."

I read it and, by God, it did. It filled up my heart with light. This was not *The Blinkies*. This was the story of a man and his burden, a burden too heavy to live with, a burden he strove to shed. For when he shed it, salvation would be his. This was *my* story, my own tortured story to find artistic fulfillment!

That is how I came to film *The Pilgrim's Progress*. And for the first time in my life, I felt as if honest achievement and self-respect were within my grasp. That night, as I shut my eyes to go to sleep, I saw a scene in the future:

I was clutching something. It was not the Academy Award or the New York Film Critics Award for Best Director. It was a paper titled, "Why *The Pilgrim's Progress* Is So Much Better than Anything Berthold Leithauser Ever Did, It Makes Me Laugh." The report was by my daughter, Somerset.

FROM FRIAR CURRIE'S JOURNAL

October 31, 1982

Ferris has decided to film *The Pilgrim's Progress*. He will not be sorry! Hot dog! I think my time out here will truly make a difference.

But I will say this: it takes a long time to get a project going in Hollywood. It has already been three weeks.

CHAPTER 6

BASED UPON: *THE PILGRIM'S PROGRESS*

DIANE ASADORIAN, Professor of Seventeenth Century
English Literature, Columbia University

I've devoted my whole career to the study of *The Pilgrim's
Progress* and even I found the idea of a movie unimaginable.
To get a kick out of *The Progress,* one must have a
thorough grounding in semiotics, semantics, pragmatics,
and syntactics—that's the key to fun. But for people who
aren't into that, and that would include—well, of course,
I'm speaking roughly now, just sort of rounding it off,
you know—but I think that would include almost one
hundred percent of the people now living in this country,
The Progress is a highly questionable source for a film. In
essence, it's a heavy-handed religious allegory with a
story of such plodding repetition and lifelessness that if it
happened to you and you wanted to tell someone about
it, you would risk losing their friendship. Now, of course,
that's the kind of story that really holds me, but I think it's
safe to say that most people don't go for that. Certainly no
one who has read it likes it. To be honest, I can't imagine
how it survived through the ages.

CORBY GARRISON, editor, *Cliffs Notes*

For years we have had letters from students begging us to do *The Pilgrim's Progress*. For a while, we tried, but none of our readers could get through it. We finally called in a specialist, Miss Meserole, who had handled the Venerable Bede's *Ecclesiastical History of the English People* for us. She's the toughest tool we've got. She broke down ten pages from the end, overcome by Eye Lock, a condition where the eyes refuse to move any further and one's sight blurs.

That's when we washed our hands of *The Pilgrim's Progress*. If Miss Meserole couldn't crack it, no one could.

JULIA SCHWERDLOFF BUSH

Obviously, we should never have let Bucky run the studio. But the only way we could've convinced him that he didn't have the ability to run it was to tell him we'd secretly been supporting his other businesses all these years. I just couldn't bring myself to tell him the truth like that. After all those years of lying, it seemed immoral. I thought the best thing for all of us was to let him go ahead with this movie but that we take certain steps to protect ourselves.

Meelie suggested that we put someone in the studio to help Bucky make a success of things. She felt that the only chance of success, if there was any, was to have someone there who would keep Bucky out of every decision, leaving him, well, I'm ashamed to say, totally powerless. I said that would be okay as long as Bucky didn't know.

EXCERPT FROM "SPERGYLE STEPS IN AT SCHWERDLOFF,"
VARIETY, NOVEMBER 5, 1982

. . . The 32-year-old Ike Spergyle, who has been responsible for turning around MGM, Fox, Universal, Columbia, Paramount, and Warner Brothers, has recently been appointed to head the Mr. Schwerdloff Studio, where he will report directly to Bucky Schwerdloff. If anyone can save the Mr. Schwerdloff Studio, it is believed to be he.

Ike Spergyle is obsessive about work. When he

came to the ailing MGM in 1979, he arrived at the studio at 7:00 A.M. The other executives didn't arrive until 9:00 A.M. The next day, everyone was there at 7:00 A.M. The following day, Spergyle came at 6:30, and then at 4:30, and then at 1:30, until finally he passed himself and gained a day. Later, when his doctor advised him that he wasn't getting enough rest, Spergyle hired someone to sleep for him.

He is famous for keeping films on schedule and under budget, a longtime problem at the Schwerdloff Studio. "He knows how to get the most out of people," said a studio executive who wished to remain anonymous. When a stuntman refused to jump from the fifty-ninth floor of the Empire State Building to the hood of a moving cab in the Burt Reynolds starrer *Slaphappy*, Spergyle is said to have withheld the man's epilepsy medication until he complied.

Spergyle has pushed for years to automate the industry. "Except for some of the actors," he once said, "I can't think of a job in this business that couldn't be done more economically by a robot. If a machine can make coffee, it can certainly put makeup on someone."

Spergyle said he is "looking forward" to working with the people at the Schwerdloff Studio.

BUCKY SCHWERDLOFF

I couldn't believe it. Ike Spergyle—*the* Ike Spergyle—called me and said he wanted to work for me. He said it would be an honor. I was so excited. Everyone wanted to get on the bandwagon!

IKE SPERGYLE

Re: my first meeting with Bucky, I was apprehensive. In our telephone conversations, Amelia had given me the impression that he was completely unconnected to reality. I was afraid that when I walked in I might find him trying to feed a doughnut to the stapler. On the contrary, I found him to be a reasonable, agreeable man. I foresaw no trouble in controlling him.

Bucky was the variable about which I had been most worried. Certainly I wasn't worried about Keneally. He was the King of the Box Office. He had just completed a breakdown and he was coming in for a meeting. Bucky and I were to meet with him that morning, during which time he was going to tell us the story, as neither Bucky nor I had read the book. Our story department assessed *The Pilgrim's Progress* as a boring, artsy, uncommercial property, but I was confident Keneally could turn it into gold.

EXCERPTS FROM TAPED STORY MEETING, NOVEMBER 29, 1982

[Schwerdloff taped the meeting, preferring a taped record to his own notes. Present were Schwerdloff, Keneally, and Spergyle. A few minutes of pleasantries were followed by:]

SPERGYLE: May we hear the story then?
KENEALLY: Certainly. We open on our hero, Christian, who is leaving the City of Destruction. He is, like

all of us, trying to find Salvation. He carries on his back a great Burden. We never know what exactly the Burden is. It is the burden we all carry with us, each and every day. Perhaps it is the burden of our parents' expectations or of being the youngest student at a major Ivy League institution, one which many consider the most rigorous in the country, and I don't mean Yale or Princeton. Perhaps it is the burden of fearing that every woman who loves you, loves you because of the roles you can get her, not because of the type of man you are.

SCHWERDLOFF: Could the burden be luggage?

KENEALLY: (laughs) Very amusing, Bucky; it's going to be jolly working with you. Now, Christian hooks up with two fellows, Obstinate and Pliable, but is only able to persuade Pliable to go along. Obstinate is, well, too stubborn. So off Pliable and Christian go to find Salvation, but, before they know it, they fall into the Slough of Despond. Well, this is too much for Pliable, but Christian is made of tougher stuff and goes ahead.

SPERGYLE: I apologize for interrupting, but . . . are these the names you intend to use?

KENEALLY: These are the names in the book.

SPERGYLE: You don't think the names tip the story? You think it's a surprise that Pliable is the one who is persuaded to go with Christian and Obstinate refuses?

KENEALLY: This isn't a movie of suspense or wondering what will happen.

SPERGYLE: It's just that you do suspense so well.

KENEALLY: Exactly. And I don't want to do what I do well. I've already done that.

SPERGYLE: (clearing throat) Very admirable. Spoken as an artist.

KENEALLY: I *am* an artist.

SPERGYLE: Yes. And I'm looking forward to hearing the rest of the story—though I'm not in any suspense, which was your goal, I believe, and one you've achieved.

KENEALLY: Now, before Christian can get to Morality . . .

[For the next hour, Keneally recounted the rest of the plot: Christian's troubles on Difficulty Hill; the embarrassments endured in the Valley of Humiliation; his encounters with Faithful, Talkative, Mr. Moneylove. There is much, much more but it is unendurable to describe. At the story's conclusion:]

SPERGYLE: Let me, if I might, bring up the vulgar question of how we're going to sell this movie. It is clearly not like your others. There is very little action and no humor.

KENEALLY: It's an art film. I suggest you sell it by quoting the reviews.

SPERGYLE: But most art films do not cost $15 million, as you project this will. I suggest that, for purposes of ensuring our investment, we use some big names. What stars would be right?

SCHWERDLOFF: Oh, yeah, let's get some stars!

KENEALLY: Oh, no. No, no, no, no, no, no, no, no.

SPERGYLE: No stars?

KENEALLY: It's not that I'm against stars. It's just that I don't want to divert the audience's attention from the meanings in the story. But, look, I don't mean to be contentious. Let's get some stars. I just don't think we should mention in the publicity or the credits that they are involved; and we'll devise, I don't know, masks or something to disguise them. That I'd allow.

SPERGYLE: I see.

KENEALLY: Now look, look here. Let me tell you something that should give you all the confidence you'll need. I have never had my heart in any of the movies I've directed. I have my heart in this.

SCHWERDLOFF: So let me ask you something. Do you definitely want to do this movie? Because I have an idea I think you're going to like better. Plus it's my own idea, so we don't have to spend money and buy the book like we would with your idea. My movie's called *Countdown*. It's about parents who get younger than their kids.

KENEALLY: Younger than . . . ? How would that work?

SCHWERDLOFF: I don't know . . . some accident . . . maybe something with a sunlamp or something . . . I think it's very commercial.

KENEALLY: I think we're trying for something a little higher than that, aren't we, Ike?

SPERGYLE: Well . . .

KENEALLY: Very well, then, is that all we—

SCHWERDLOFF: Wait. I'm just thinking a little about the budget myself now. What year is this movie in? Are we going to have to get those old cars?

SPERGYLE and KENEALLY: No.

SCHWERDLOFF: Well, this is great! I've always loved the Pilgrims, and Thanksgiving is my favorite holiday. Hey, that's a good omen! And, did you guys know that at the first Thanksgiving, the Pilgrims didn't have turkey? They had eggs. I can't remember where I heard that but it's true.

SPERGYLE: (whispering) Mr. Keneally, could you slip me a piece of paper with your numbers and I'll give you mine. It's best not to bother Bucky with—

SCHWERDLOFF: You know, I decided I would close the studio unless I got Ferris Keneally and a big blockbuster movie. Looks like I got both.

WE'RE MAKING *PROGRESS* AT THE MR. SCHWERDLOFF STUDIO

The Mr. Schwerdloff Studio is excited to announce that Ferris Keneally, whose last film, *The Blinkies*, was the top-grossing summer film of 1982, will direct his new film *The Pilgrim's Progress* for us.

The Pilgrim's Progress: Give Thanks for It Everywhere, Summer of '83.

CHAPTER 7

"LIGHTS, CAMERA . . ."

IKE SPERGYLE

Many people have asked me why I didn't kill the project the minute I heard it. After all, it was completely unsuited to the screen. Agreed. However, Ferris Keneally had never made a failure. Every picture he made was a top-grosser, no matter how bad the script was.

Furthermore, I was haunted by a mistake I had made years before vis-à-vis Keneally. I was at Universal and a film of his, *Planet Hoppers*, was submitted to me. I rejected it. I thought the story was heavy-handed and the characters were ones an audience wouldn't relate to. *Planet Hoppers* went to Paramount, where, as everyone knows, it became the top-grossing film of the year. I've had to live with that every day since then.

I knew *Pilgrim's Progress* was going to be a bomb. But I knew *Planet Hoppers* was going to be a bomb. I couldn't afford to keep canceling bombs that grossed $100 million.

. . .

BELIEVING THAT "CREATIVITY IS BEST SERVED WHEN IT CAN BE EASILY FILED," SPERGYLE INSISTED ON A DETAILED ACCOUNTING OF ALL DECISIONS. THE NUMEROUS FORMS HE DEVISED IN THIS INTEREST ARE LEGENDARY IN HOLLYWOOD.*

MEMO

FROM: Ike Spergyle   DATE: December 25, 1982
TO: Ferris Keneally   SUBJECT: The Pilgrim's Progress

Dear Mr. Keneally,

We're all:
(x) excited
( ) concerned
( ) alarmed

about your project, The Pilgrim's Progress, henceforth known as XA573 . Attached please find form relating to:

(x) suggested screenwriters
( ) script changes
( ) expense vouchers
( ) letter indicating termination of your services and name of your replacement.

Please fill out the attached form immediately at your convenience.

(x) Looking forward to working with you.
( ) Keep up the good work.
( ) Sorry things didn't work out.
( ) Our lawyers will be in touch.

With warmest personal regards,

Ike Spergyle

*For an exhaustive study of Mr. Spergyle's forms, see To:/From: The Forms of Ike Spergyle, edited by Rudy Behlmer, Viking, 1979.

Form SSW1 P6

Hi! Your movie needs a screenwriter! Below are their bios. Please read and then won't you help by filling in the enclosed *Screenwriter Ability Grid*? Remember, please press hard as you'll be making fifteen copies! Thanks!

HOLLY HULSE
Emmy winner for the "Rhoda's Mother Takes Exercise Class with Mary" episode on *The Mary Tyler Moore Show*. Also wrote the Goldie Hawn film *Water Girl*. Can make anything funny.

SARAH JANE MARTIN
Wrote *Mrs. Welch, Madame Governor, Beth*, etc. Holds the record for most Oscar nominations without ever having won one. Does not use any form of mechanized transportation. Allow ample time for her to get to meetings.

TOM HELM, STEVE BIGGS, WADE DAVIS
Wrote National Lampoon's *LaMaze Class*, the Richard Pryor/John Candy film *Foreign Legion*, and Chevy Chase's *Mayor Nincompoop*. Agent says they want to do a Pilgrim movie.

HUNTER LA PORTE
Won National Rifle Association's Best Screenplay award for Chuck Norris film *Hotshot*. Also scripted Arnold Schwarzenegger's *Bicep* and Charles Bronson's *H*O*R*N*E*T*. Wrote first draft of *On Golden Pond*. This later rewritten—very little of La Porte's material remained. Writes quickly.

VICTORIA ROSTOW AND JOSE BERICAL
Wrote *Circumstantial Evidence, Corridors of Power,*

and *The Truth, The Whole Truth, and Nothing But The Truth, So Help You God*. Feel *Pilgrim's Progress* can be updated to dramatize death of '60s idealism, sinister growth of corporations, and possibly plight of farmers. Also see good love story potential. Not good on one-liners.

Please rate from 1 to 10 (10 is best)

	HULSE	MARTIN	LA PORTE	ROSTOW, BERICA	HELM, BIGGS DAVIS
story sense					
ability to write believable characters					
dialogue skills					
number of films to gross in excess of $50 million					
ability to understand a change the studio wants even if the studio can't exactly say it					
willingness to put in crash scenes					
your feeling that screen-writer is not above use of flashbacks					
willingness to sacrifice life for film (just guess)					
Total					

December 28, 1982

Dearest old Ike,

You are the kindest, sweetest, swellest fellow. Most obliged for the list of suggested screenwriters which arrived in the A.M. post. Was all settled in and ready to review it when, damn!, the dog got it. Not to worry—am in touch with several top writers, all of whom have the credentials a film of this quality demands. Stay tan!

Yours,

F.

FERRIS KENEALLY'S LIST OF POSSIBLE SCREENWRITERS

Ones I've Heard From—Pros and Cons

Isaac B. Singer
Positive: won Nobel Prize.
Negative: wants to adapt to Yiddish short story.
Vladimir Yushenka
Negative: imprisoned behind Iron Curtain.
Positive: works cheap.
Tom Stoppard
Positive: superb writer, great at dialogue and story, witty, pithy, acerbic, deep.
Negative: has written for screen before.
Alice Walker
Negative: wants to change story and call it *On the Road to Our Mother's House*. Her notes say: ". . . about a woman, Woman, who is shack-

led by the Burden of a patriarchal society. Woman walks down a long, muddy road, lined with men who throw rocks against her face and push themselves against her place, her woman's place, and Woman runs away and falls into the Slough of their Hate. She is rescued by the Angel of Sisters who kisses Woman on the lips, full and hard and sweet, and makes Woman see that life is not good on that road. Then Angel takes Woman to Another Road, a lilac-scented road which leads to her mother's house—and all our mothers' houses.''

Positive: always good to have a woman around in case a button comes off or we need a sauce for something.

Günter Grasse

Negative: from his letter: ''. . . I love that Slough of Despond, that's just the best! So what I'd like to do is have Christian, right in the beginning, fall in the Slough. But then, instead of surviving as he does in the book and going on to have many pages of adventures, let's drown him. And then, and this is the thing I'm really excited about, let's have the movie fade to black and stay that way for two hours. This will confront the audience with what it will look at all the time if it continues to do nothing to rid the world of nuclear weapons. Every twenty minutes or so, a rat could run across the screen. We can play with those times.''

Positive: has his own car.

KENEALLY EVENTUALLY REJECTED ALL OF THE AUTHORS ON HIS LIST. HIS LAST CHOICE, LILLIAN HELLMAN, DECLINED THE PROJECT.

January 29, 1983

Dear Mr. Keneally,

Perhaps you thought of me for your movie because of the admirable stand I took against McCarthyism in the fifties when I told a hushed Senate chamber, "I cannot and will not cut my conscience to fit this year's fashions." Or perhaps you were thinking of the time I took a bullet in the nose protecting Dash in a prison riot or the incident in which I traveled to Cambodia and single-handedly enforced a cease-fire. If you doubt the veracity of these episodes, as someone has, each and every one can be verified by checking my diaries where I wrote them all down, exactly as they happened.

I am very sorry to say I must decline your offer. You need someone who can write stirringly about heroism and I can only write about heroism when it is my own.

Sincerely,

Lillian Hellman

UNABLE TO FIND A WRITER HE LIKED, KENEALLY DECIDED TO WRITE THE SCREENPLAY HIMSELF.

Ferris,

Really glad you're going to write the script. Can I
make a suggestion? I always think it's funny in a movie
when a man has trouble in the kitchen. Maybe Christian makes dinner for Discretion and puts too much
rice in the pot. Maybe he cooks it in a pressure
cooker?
    Call if you need anything.

                                                   Bucky

MEMO

FROM: Ike Spergyle   DATE: February 4, 1983
TO: Ferris Keneally   SUBJECT: XA573

Dear Ferris,

Received notification of your intention to write XA573
yourself. We are all delighted with your decision. We
feel you will make XA573 a film all audiences will
want to see.

    In ordinary circumstances we require at this point
that the story go through a complicated screening
process where the screenwriter pitches his story to seven
levels of listeners, concluding with myself and Mr.
Schwerdloff. At any point, of course, he may be asked
to stop and possibly leave. In your case, however,
because of your experience and our desire not to waste
your valuable time, these preliminary steps may be
bypassed. For the sake of our records, however, we
will require that you fill out the enclosed waiver forms

113

so that our computer does not at a later date cancel your project and notify guards to have you removed from the lot.

Waiver Forms #1 and #4, as indicated, should be typed. Waiver Forms #2 and #5 should be handwritten in bold roman lettering only. Waiver Forms #3 and #6 should be in a pretty cursive, but we request that you use the printed "Q" ("Q") rather than the cursive "Q" ("2") as our computer misreads the latter as a "two" ("2").

This leaves only Form #7. We require a thirty-page—please be exact—single-spaced plot synopsis. Each character's name should be typed in a different color. Sentences should be concluded on the same line they started. Pages should be Scotch-guarded to protect them from coffee stains and fire.

With warmest personal regards,

Ike Spergyle

cc: Bucky Schwerdloff
Waiver Department

FROM IKE SPERGYLE TO FERRIS KENEALLY

February 4, 1983

Mr. Keneally,

After several nights of sleeping on the matter, I remain concerned about the character names in *The Pilgrim's Progress*: Mr. Hate-Light, Superstition, Lord Desire of Vainglory, etc. It was my fear that these names are not in vogue as much today as they were in 1678, the year *The Pilgrim's Progress* was published.

Not content to rely on my own instincts in such an important matter, I had our research department conduct a phone poll asking people whether they would see a movie with characters named Obstinate, Pliable, Sloth, etc. Everyone said "no," except for one man named "Bubba." One reason people go to movies is because they think they have a chance of hearing their own names said by a movie star. Research shows that most of today's movie-viewing audience are between the ages of fifteen and twenty-one; that is, people born between the years 1963–69. Michelle Smith's *Popular Names* states that the most popular names during those years were John, Michael, Andrew, Alexander, Ringo, and Caroline, Barbara, Cathy, Flower, and Susan. We feel that it would add immeasurably to our box-office potential if you would use only these names.

With warmest personal regards,

Ike Spergyle

FROM FERRIS KENEALLY TO IKE SPERGYLE

February 8, 1983

Ike,

Nice fat packet from you today. Didn't open. Know it was only more of your good words and kind encouragement. Am racing to pack. Off to merry England where will write swell screenplay and scout locations.

You're a peach. First glass of ale will be lifted to you. I like Ike!

F.

6/6/83

PIP, PIP! HAVE FINISHED THE SCRIPT AND IT'S A DILLY. WILL WAIT TO SEND IT AS OVERSEAS COSTS ARE SKYHIGH AND AM LOATHE TO RUN UP THE STUDIO TAB. BAD NEWS THOUGH. SCOUTED AROUND AND ENGLAND DOES NOT LOOK LIKE IT USED TO, AT LEAST THE WAY IT DID WHEN MGM BUILT IT FOR *NATIONAL VELVET*. ENGLAND LOOKS LIKE FRANCE. AM FLYING TO FRANCE WHERE I HOPE THINGS WILL LOOK MORE LIKE ENGLAND. ALL THE BEST, F. P.S. AM SORRY NOT TO HAVE BEEN IN TOUCH FEB, MAR, APR, AND MAY BUT HAD A BIT OF WRITER'S BLOCK. CAME OUT OF IT WHEN I REMEMBERED "I MATTER!" THE BEST WAY TO SHOW MYSELF THAT I MATTER IS TO BUY MYSELF THINGS. BILLS TO FOLLOW.

June 28, 1983

Bucky,

A curious item has come to my attention from accounting. Can you clarify the attached?

Ike Spergyle

P.S. You say Keneally has finished script. Do you have it?

AMOUNT	TYPE OF ITEM	COST	
1	Double-decker bus coffee mug	$3.25	
1	Cadbury Yorkville "Crunchy"	$0.75	
1	Canterbury Cathedral	$12,225,698.00	
Total		$12,225,702.00	

FROM FERRIS KENEALLY TO DR. YALE ZIMET

June 8, 1983

Dear Doc,

Life is perfect at last. I have fallen in love with a woman I met here in Paris. Her name is Simone Bejour. She takes deaf people through the Jeu de Pomme. She makes me wish I were deaf!

She is an exquisite beauty and a simple person. She does not look down on me as Claire does as she knows nothing of my success in films. This is the most important development because it sets her apart from so many of the women in Hollywood: she loves me not for what I've done but for who I am.

And I thank you for helping me to become who I am.

I am,

F.

Ritz Hotel

June 10, 1983

My little Treasure, my own,

I know you are only in the shower but it seems like days since I have seen you! My world is empty without you! Please hurry, my darling! I am so afraid that something will happen to you! Please do not slip and crack your head wide open on the spigot! You have the most beautiful head in the world!

F.

6/12/83

BONJOUR CHER BUCKÉ. HAVE FOUND OUR STAR! THERE IS NO PART FOR HER AS YET SO WILL RE-WRITE SCRIPT. WILL TEACH HER ENGLISH ON THE PLANE. YOU'LL LOVE HER. I DO. FERRIS. P.S. FRANCE CAN'T BE ENGLAND. LOOKS LIKE GERMANY. WILL NEED TO BUILD ENGLAND ON STUDIO LOT.

June 16, 1983

Bucky,

Have investigated Keneally's proposal to build "England" on the studio lot. Cost in excess of $40 million, not including heather.

Have learned that Texas is now cheapest state in nation in which to produce films. Have not been to Texas since 1961 so do not know how much it looks like seventeenth-century England. However, Texas Film Board very eager to accommodate us and will give us bargain rates if we agree to plug Texas in film. Think this solves our problem.

Ike Spergyle

P.S. No script. Where is script? Am becoming very anxious.

FROM BUCKY SCHWERDLOFF TO IKE SPERGYLE

June 29, 1983

Ike,

I'm going to have dinner with Ferris tonight who is back from France and I will ask him about the script. But I don't know why you want to read it so bad. It will only spoil the movie for you.

Bucky

P.S. Do you read the last page of a book first, too?

June 30, 1983

Ike,

I had a nice dinner last night with Ferris and his fiancée*
at Chasen's. He is in a great mood and treated everyone in the restaurant to their meals**. I told him about
the Texas thing we've done and he said he liked the
idea as long as they could build an England that looks
real. Meanwhile he plans to cast people right away.
 I'm so optimistic, I may try out for Hopeful!***

Bucky

*Simone Bejour
**In fact, records show Keneally charged the meals to the studio.
***The part later played by Boswell Sonnenfeld.

July 1, 1983

Dear Mr. Keneally,

I am sending this letter to you opened as you seem to
find it too much trouble to open the other letters I've
sent. None of these letters has even been acknowl-
edged, except the one which was returned to this office
spray-painted yellow. I have been writing you repeat-
edly requesting a script, an obligation on your part
which came due legally five months and three days
ago. Please submit the script immediately. And I mean
it. Now, come on!
 Additionally, could you please explain why you
bought Canterbury Cathedral? I was not aware that

there was any need for a cathedral in the picture, but, of course, I have not seen the script, and for all I know, it's about the progress some pilgrims made in building Canterbury Cathedral. However, even if there were a need for Canterbury Cathedral, why didn't you rent it?

The purchase of Canterbury Cathedral is doubly perplexing to me since you are not going to shoot any of the film in England. I hope, Mr. Keneally, you are not planning to move Canterbury Cathedral to Texas.

> Delighted to have you back.
> With warmest personal regards,
>
> Ike Spergyle

FROM FERRIS KENEALLY TO IKE SPERGYLE

July 25, 1983

Dear Ike,

Your letter was a joke, yes? I'm sure I don't have to defend my choice of Canterbury Cathedral to you—with its breathtaking stained glass that inspired the poet Shelley to write "On Standing in Front of Canterbury Cathedral and Looking at It." Wait till you hear the grand acoustics! In fact, why don't you just unplug your calculator and hop the next British Airways to London and hurry out and hear the boys' choir sing "All Things Bright and Beautiful." You've been a bit of a grouch lately and I think it might do you good.

Call me for keys and I'll make you copies—gratis!

> F.

P.S. I'm a little foggy on something. Weren't you the executive who canceled *Plant Hoppers* at Universal?

July 28, 1983

Mr. Keneally,

I am informed that the woman you have cast as the lead in your movie (I still have not seen the script) is French and speaks no English. Furthermore, from what I understand, she is not even an actress. Were I to rank the types of actors whom I would want to appear in a project that will be as difficult to market as *The Pilgrim's Progress*, I would order them thusly:

1. Stars with worldwide box office appeal
2. Stars with box office appeal in the U.S.
3. Excellent actors who have no box office appeal
4. Mechanized novelties (e.g., E.T.)
5. Animated figures
6. Foreigners who speak no English and are not actors

Therefore, until the first five options are exhausted, I must say *no* to your casting selection of Simone Bejour. Please recast and notify this office of your selection.

With warmest personal regards,

Ike Spergyle

cc: B. Schwerdloff

August 3, 1983

Ike and Ferris,

Great idea, Ike! Let's do try to get E.T. for the movie. Ferris, any parts for him? Where do they keep him? And if we get him, can I be the one that steers him?

Bucky

August 1, 1983

Bucky,

I cannot make the movie you so want me to make if Ike Spergyle continues to hover over me, questioning my every little move. He is like Hitler—his way or no way.

He will not allow Simone Bejour to be in the picture, just because she can't speak any English. You met Simone. She has qualities that don't come through in speech.

Can you help?

F.

August 6, 1983

Ferris,

I was doodling as I thought this Simone problem over and I noticed something that, in all the fuss over if she speaks English or not, everyone else has overlooked. Simone has an *s* in it, Ferris has an *s* in it, *Pilgrim's Progress* has an *s* in it (three *s*'s!), and blockbuster has an *s* in it. Good omen! Point this out to Ike. I'm sure he'll be won over. And have him meet Simone. She's cute.

Also, did you really work for Hitler? If so, could we have lunch sometime? I'd like to know if it's true he liked animals so much.

Speaking of animals, audiences *love* animals that cock their heads when they see human beings do stupid things. Let's put some of this in the movie. See Pamela Russo* about whatever you'll need.

Bucky

*Pamela Russo: Schwerdloff Studio Animal Head

• • •

MS. BEJOUR MET MR. SPERGYLE AND WAS APPROVED. SHE, KENEALLY, AND THE REST OF THE CREW LEFT FOR TEXAS A FEW DAYS LATER.

August 17, 1983

Mr. Keneally,

Though the commencement of photography of *The Pilgrim's Progress* is due to begin in two weeks, after numerous postponements, none of which has been explained to my satisfaction, we still have not received a copy of your script. Please send immediately.

Also, you will need to file a Delay Explanation Form, plus a Notice of Script Delivery Form. If you do not have these forms, *please* file a Lack of Forms Form promptly with this office. This is the final request I will make for your script. If this office has not received it within three (3) business days, the matter will be turned over to a collection agency.

With every wish for a successful start of production, and as always,

With warmest personal regards,

Ike Spergyle

cc: Bucky Schwerdloff

August 18, 1983

Dear Mr. Spergyle,

I have written you now five times requesting a copy of the script for *The Pilgrim's Progress*. Our arrangement with you provides the lowest possible rates for your company in exchange for prominent promotion of Texas within the film. I must, therefore, see the script to verify and approve the magnitude of and the manner in which Texas is promoted.

You mentioned that *The Pilgrim's Progress* takes place in a nonexistent place many centuries ago, your point being, I assume, that a plug for Texas cannot fit in. May I suggest a solution? Why not have your characters meet a traveler from Texas who could tell them all about the state, our fine schools and roads, our diverse terrain, and the new Galleria in Dallas?

You say you cannot send me a script because you allege the director has not mailed you one, even though you are his boss and pay all the bills and are due to go into production any day now. Do you think I believe this?

Yours sincerely,

Margaret Farrell

P.S. I do not.

Finally, I did obtain the script. I did not let on to Keneally that I had obtained it because I knew it would upset him.

It was unquestionably the worst script I'd ever seen—the only parts I had any hopes for were the illegible parts—the other parts were boring and/or incomprehensible. A true catastrophe. If it had been anyone else but Keneally, I would've canceled the project. But I knew that as soon as I did, he'd take it to Paramount, change the name to *Planet Hoppers II* and it would make more money than the government prints in a year.

The other thought that prevented me from firing Keneally was that although we had absolutely nothing to show for it, we had already spent $15 million on the project—the entire budget we had allotted for *The Pilgrim's Progress*—before the first day of shooting had begun. I could not let that wasted money go down the drain.

FROM FERRIS KENEALLY TO BUCKY SCHWERDLOFF

August 22, 1983

Dear Bucky,

You are the only person I can talk to about this project, this project which is so near to both our hearts. Production is scheduled to begin Monday. But if that ape that heads the studio doesn't get off my back, I don't know when it will start. If ever. He pours over every single purchase, thinking he can put a price on art. He pesters me endlessly about details, yet he himself is forgetful. He claims I never sent him a script. How vividly I recall the autumn afternoon I brought it to him. We sat in the leaves in his backyard and I read it to him. When I read the scene where the Burden of Sin falls from Christian's back, he cried so hard he tore his lip. I suppose he forgets it was I who drove him to the hospital where the doctor pulled me aside and said, "Your quick thinking probably saved Mr. Spergyle's mouth."

As you know, I have been and remain deeply mentally ill. It is imperative that I get my way on everything all the time. Is that so much to ask after I have struggled so hard to keep this film on time and under budget? Can you please arrange it so that he does not distract me during filming?

Bless you for everything.

F.

FROM IKE SPERGYLE TO BUCKY SCHWERDLOFF

August 25, 1983

Dear Bucky,

Through no fault of my own and, in fact, despite great efforts to the contrary, project XA573 is five months behind schedule and has already cost over $15 million. This is before a single inch of film has been shot. Not one of us, including myself, has seen a script. I don't care what he says about my lip. It is not torn. It has never been torn. There would be a mark if it were torn and there is no mark. Come look at it. See for yourself.

Clearly, Keneally will not allow me on the set. Clearly, we must have an executive producer on the set to watch over him and alert us when there is trouble. This will be difficult as he will perceive any outsider as a threat. Can you think of someone who might work out?

Looking forward to shooting day #1. Think we've got a winner!

With warmest personal regards,

Ike Spergyle

BUCKY SCHWERDLOFF

I saw right away that Ike and Ferris weren't getting along. I had to find someone quickly who could make everyone get along. Immediately I thought of Friar Currie. In those days, he could still get along with people.

Friar Currie was working for the studio as a beggar then. He used to stand on Santa Monica Boulevard with a cup saying, "Please give to the Mr. Schwerdloff Studio!" He was very convincing—a couple of times, I found myself contributing. He usually brought in sixteen, seventeen, eighteen dollars. At this time this was our only money coming in, so it was a risk for me to take him off that job. But you know me, I'm a risker. Currie was the only person both Ike and Ferris would allow to be executive producer. They both thought he would do whatever they told him. That's how Friar Currie came to be executive producer.

Here's the thing: I worked on the script for a long time, trying to adapt *The Pilgrim's Progress* in a conventional way, but I just couldn't get anywhere with it. It didn't, well—the thing didn't sing. I had wanted to make a small, personal film and this was simply not personal enough.

I was attracted to *The Pilgrim's Progress* because it dealt with a man who was having a life crisis, which, as everyone knows, I was, too. But the specifics Bunyan used, I realized, were not ones a modern audience could relate to. So I used the idea behind *The Pilgrim's Progress*—an allegorical study of a man's struggle to find happiness—but modernized it, changed the life crisis to my own and the main character to me. And the title, of course, I had to change the title.

The movie, then, *My Progress,* was not only a creative exercise for me but a therapeutic one. In it, I examined events in my life that Dr. Zimet felt I had put off for too long and were important to confront. In so doing I could exorcise the demons of my past, and just as the character in the movie could find happiness, so, too, could I.

The structure of the film was simple. It was a trip I took through my life. As the movie opens, we hear a train. We do not see it for a long, long time. Then, slowly, it rolls into view. It is all of it empty; through window after window we see car after car of empty seats. Then there is the last car. There in the last car sits Terrence, an artist. Terrence represents me. In the seat opposite Terrence is a dove. The dove represents his talent. The dove is in a cage.

Terrence is thinking about the dove. The train pulls out of frame. The camera tilts to show the train climbing a steep hill and being swallowed by a fog, the fog of memory. The train has set out on a journey through Terrence's life, making stops at different points in his past. At each of the stops, Terrence tries to come to terms with various crises in his life.

I don't believe in labeling, but if you were going to label *My Progress,* I think you'd have to call it a "surreal psycho-docu-travelogue."

I kept the script away from the studio heads because I didn't want them meddling with it. When Friar Currie came down to executive produce, I knew that he'd be upset with the changes—he had told me that my filming *The Pilgrim's Progress* had fulfilled his every wish—so I could never bring myself to tell him I'd changed it.

Ultimately, I couldn't be worried about the friar. This was my film, I was determined to see that it came out exactly as I wanted it.

FROM FRIAR CURRIE'S JOURNAL

August 29, 1983

Life is abundantly good. Bucky has asked me to be "executive producer" of the movie enactment of *The Pilgrim's Progress.* I do not know exactly what an executive producer does but I think it is like being a shepherd.

I placed a telephone call to Father Abbot to tell him of my good fortune. He told me of the time many years ago when a group of Hermits dramatized the saga of the Salt Lake City Scrolls*.

In the dramatized version, the Communitarians disguised themselves as rocks instead of logs. As soon as he saw this, Flann Washburn demanded the end of the enactment. He said, "Every story has a meaning. If you change the story, you change the meaning!" So that the dramatist and director would always remember that truth rings clear like a bell and that lies are a heavy burden upon one's shoulders, Washburn commanded the two Communitarians who had written the enactment to walk around the yard all day with the bell from the chapel tower upon their shoulders.

I shall remember this lesson. I shall shepherd the book to the screen—this book which, outside the *Bible*, has had the greatest influence over my life—and I will take care that nothing happens to it on its way.

*According to the legend of the Salt Lake City scrolls, the Communitarians, in their search for a home, stopped in Salt Lake City. One night around their campfire, they read aloud from the Communitarian Commandments, which Flann Washburn himself had written in beautiful script on a papyrus scroll. In the distance, they heard the approach of a gang of Mormon roughnecks with whom they had already had trouble. The Communitarians quickly disguised themselves as a pile of logs and went undetected by the Mormons. However, in their panic, the Communitarians had left the Scroll of Commandments by the fire. It was discovered by the rampaging Mormons, who read it and laughed and threw it in Salt Lake. When the Mormons left, the Communitarians dived into the lake and retrieved their cherished scroll. Though it had been in the water for several hours before being discovered, miraculously, the scroll was bone dry.

CHAPTER 8

"ACTION!"

AMELIA SCHWERDLOFF DUFFEE

I had to tip my hat to him. Buck had gotten Ferris Keneally to do a movie for the studio. I called up Julia to see how much money we were paying Keneally but Buck'd done it all on his own. Hell of a catch! There was a big article in the *L.A. Times* about Buck called "The Rising Son." The stock went up ten points the day Buck'd signed Keneally. The next day the paper ran a follow-up: "The Stock Also Rises."

I had lunch with Julia that day. We couldn't stop laughing—when we thought of Buck, who had failed at everything, being so successful in the movie business, a business where failure is the norm. Julia even said, "Maybe show business is really his calling! I've certainly never seen him happier."

THE *PROGRESS* CREW ARRIVED IN MARFA, TEXAS, ON AUGUST 10, 1983. THE TOWN WENT ALL OUT FOR THEIR ARRIVAL. UNAWARE THAT THE FILM WAS NO LONGER TO BE *THE PILGRIM'S PROGRESS*, THIS AD APPEARED IN THE *MARFA MORNING CRIER*:

THE MARFA BULLDOGS WELCOME
THE HOLLYWOOD PILGRIMS!!

Here's To A Super "Kickoff"
Of Your Movie!

S * C * H * E * D * U * L * E   O * F   A * L * L
E * V * E * N * T * S

12 (Noon!)
Come And Get Your Own Barbe-Que (delicious!)
At the Petroleum Club of Marfa.

1:30
Watermelon Roll out back at the Blakemore's.

2:30–6
"Our Texas" (Musical enactment of the history of
Texas with batons.) Marfa High Sch. Rbt. E. Lee
Auditorium.

6:30
Box dinner at Dennis the Menace Park. (Tambou-
rine music by "Tambourines Over Texas.")

8:00
Marfa Bulldogs vs. The Permian Panthers. ("We'll
skin the Panthers!")

10:30–!
Victory Beer Dunk at the Marfa Tree.

S*E*E Y'A*L*L T*H*E*R*E!!!!!!!

August 30, 1983

1. Show Wall Street the studio knows what it's doing. Take out ad in *Wall Street Journal* that says, "In 1983 and 1984, the Mr. Schwerdloff Studio will only make one movie—because we want to get it right!"

2. Get lots of police cars to park outside our gates with their sirens on. This will get people interested in the studio.

3. Reinvent the whole idea of going to the movies. No ideas on this yet.

4. People miss some of every movie when they blink. Anything we can do about this problem?

5. Some publicity ideas for *Pilgrim's Progress*:

   a.) See if we can get a Pilgrim and Indian float in the Macy's Thanksgiving Day Parade.

   b.) Find out who to talk to to see about giving tomahawks to first 500 customers to movie. Let's try to get real ones. People hate gimmicks.

IKE SPERGYLE

I was never able fully to supervise the Keneally film as I had to spend so much time derailing Bucky's various projects. Maybe I should have let him go to Texas after all. He couldn't have made things there any worse.

SHOOTING REPORT

TO: Ike Spergyle   DATE: 9/1/83
FROM: Howie Perlmutter (Unit mgr.) SUBJECT: XA573

SHOOTING DAY # ___1___

Shooting canceled by Keneally, who spent 5 hours trying to light Bejour but could not because of problems lighting her nose. Stopped when Keneally decided the lights were not at fault, Bejour's nose was. So—wait till you hear this—Keneally shut down production for two weeks so Bejour could leave and get a nose job *in New York*. I'm not kidding.

At the end of the first day, we're 15 days behind schedule.

FROM FRIAR CURRIE'S JOURNAL

September 1, 1983

And it was morning of the first day but no filming took place. There were technical problems and I am ignorant of their nature.

But this thing I know: the costumes that the actors wear are modern costumes and that is not right. I told this to Ferris and he said I should not worry my little head because it would all be fixed in the editing.

Still, I was suspicious. And I said, "May I see a script?" and he said, "No."

Now I called Ike to tell him that Ferris was canceling production. Telling on the director is one of the tasks of the producer. Ike cursed the heavens and hung up the phone with great loudness. If this peeves him, wait until he hears about the modern costumes!

Such yelling frightens me. The only other time I have heard such noise is on Hermit Pride Day when we give the cry that Flann Washburn and his followers gave as they crossed the border into California*.

It might cheer me to give the cry now, even though I am no longer a Hermit.

*Here come the Hermits
Choo-choo down the track
We're puttin' on steam
And we're never comin' back!
Goooood-bye!
Goooood-bye!

IKE SPERGYLE

It was already a terrible day by the time Currie called. Bucky had come into my office first thing and said, "I've started thinking about what the studio should do after *The Pilgrim's Progress* and last night—well, you'd better just brace yourself for how great this is. It would be a movie called *That's Mr. Schwerdloff!* It would be a—oh, what do you call it? A clipping? A hodgepodge? A snack pack?"

I said, "A compilation?" and he said, "No, not exactly in a pile. It would be a collection of the best numbers from the best musicals made at the Mr. Schwerdloff Studio."

This was an appalling idea for many reasons, among them, but not restricted to, these: one, the Mr. Schwerdloff Studio had only made two musicals and, two, Bucky wanted the film to be narrated by Gene Kelly and Judy Garland. This was an equally appalling idea because: a.) Gene Kelly was an arch-enemy of Schwerdloff's; and b.) Judy Garland was dead.

Bucky's sisters had warned me that Bucky was especially thin-skinned so I phrased my answer with extreme gentleness. I said, "Bucky, that's an excellent idea. But does it bother you that because the studio has only made two musicals the film might only be a half an hour long?"

He said, "*Hogan's Heroes* is only a half-hour. I love that show. So the length isn't a problem. It's a great idea, don't you think? Don't you think we should do it?"

I said, "Yes, it's an excellent idea. But does it bother

you that Gene Kelly has never been in a movie at this studio?"

He said, "Well, now he would be! It's a great idea, don't you think? Don't you think we should do it?"

We talked about it all morning. It was clear to me that Bucky wasn't going to leave my office until I'd given the project my blessing. However, as a professional in this business, with a reputation to think of, I simply could not approve it. I'd be laughed out of town. Therefore, I said, "Bucky, I think it's a great idea but I don't think it will work. Obviously you can go ahead if you want to, but I wouldn't be doing my job if I didn't tell you I had serious reservations about the project."

His reaction was astounding. He glared at me and then he looked away and his face turned bright red. Then he started yanking his hair. Then he started kicking my desk. A grown man! I couldn't believe it!

Then I had an idea. I said, "Wait a minute. Do you mean to suggest we compile all the best musical numbers from the Mr. Schwerdloff musicals into one movie?" And he said, "Yes, that's what I've been saying."

I said, "That's a great idea! But it was already done, five years ago. It was called Sing, Mr. Schwerdloff, Sing!"

Bucky said, "Oh, too bad!" and looked disappointed. I said, "It was a huge hit, very popular." Then Bucky grinned and said, "I knew it was a great idea!"

Just as I had finally gotten Bucky out of my office, the phone rang. It was the friar telling me production had been suspended for two weeks. I'm afraid I was quite abrupt with the friar. But I was angry. When a production is shut down temporarily, the studio is obligated to continue paying every single person involved with the project. While costs continue to escalate, no product is being turned out in return. Keneally was taking advantage of the studio and it infuriated me. I could not allow this to happen.

140

So I called Keneally and told him that the studio would not allow him to suspend production and to get on with it. Keneally insisted on fixing Ms. Bejour's nose. I suggested he use a Claymation nose*. He refused. I said shoot around her. He refused. I could not control my temper. I started to yell. I said if he didn't shoot around her, we were canceling the whole project, and we would haul him into court for breach of contract and sue him for every penny he was worth.

Just then Bucky walked in again. I had to change my tone immediately. I said, "Thanks for the good news, Ferris! We're all delighted to have you aboard! Keep up the good work!"

---

*Animated clay process.

FERRIS KENEALLY

One of the most disturbing features about working for Ike was the inconsistency of his criticism. One minute he was canceling the project, the next he was praising you to the hilt. Clearly he was schizophrenic, a very unstable man—or men.

As one sympathetic to the sufferers of mental illness, I did not wish to aggravate Ike's condition, so I agreed not to suspend production.

SHOOTING REPORT

TO: *Ike Spergyle*   DATE: *9/23/83*
FROM: *Howie Perlmutter (Unit mgr.)*   SUBJECT: *XA573*

SHOOTING DAY # __2__

Scheduled to shoot exteriors.
No shooting done all day. Keneally was not happy with the clouds. He said they contradicted the mood of the scene. Yeah, right. As if people are going to tell their friends, "Don't see that movie! The clouds are terrible!"

TO: Ike Spergyle   *DATE: 10/27/83*
FROM: Howie Perlmutter (Unit mgr.)   SUBJECT: XA573

SHOOTING DAY #   __26__

   Bejour returned to work today. No scenes were
shot with her as Keneally now thinks her nose is—get
this— "tilted." Leo tried to tilt the sets to balance it out
but jugs kept falling. If you can believe it, Keneally is
sending her back to the hospital.
   It's okay with me. One of the actresses is teaching
me to knit. She said I should start with crochet because
knitting takes longer to learn, but something tells me I'll
have the time.

IKE SPERGYLE

We were having problems in every direction. One of the actors was so upset by Keneally he complained to SAG*, which, in turn, filed a suit against the studio.

FROM THE TESTIMONY OF ALEXANDER JOHNS,
ACTOR, TO THE SAG ATTORNEY

Mr. Keneally insisted we stay in character the whole time we were doing the movie. One night we all went to Sambo's Pancake House. When the waitress came, I said, "Yes, please, I'd like the—" but Mr. Keneally told me that I was not to break character until the end of the film or I'd lose my job. This was a pretty harsh thing to ask me to do since I was playing Mr. Cruelty, but what can you do? You don't want to get a reputation for being difficult.

So, there was the poor waitress looking at me, this stooped, gray-haired old woman who had told us she was only doing this until her Social Security checks started up again, and she said, "Sir, may I take your order, please?" I said, "Yeah, Granny, write this down! Two blueberry pancakes and sausage! You got that?"

She was arthritic, it was very hard for her to write, but finally she said, "Yes, sir," and I said, "Well, forget it! I've changed my mind! Give me strawberry pan-

*Screen Actors Guild

cakes and bacon!" I did this about five times—five or six, I can't remember—until I got her to cry.

When our food came, someone asked me to pass the syrup. Mr. Keneally stopped me and asked, "How would Mr. Cruelty pass the syrup?" So I spat in it. Poor Catherine Duke. She was playing Blind Faith. She had to eat it.

On our way out, I pulled the manager aside and told him that our waitress had offered to take ten dollars off our check if we paid her five. He fired her on the spot. She burst into tears and started to run out of the restaurant. Mr. Keneally was looking at me, so I tripped her.

Since the film was going so great, I thought I ought to get the other parts of the studio in shape. My most exciting project was the Movie Modernization Program. I had noticed that we weren't making nearly as much money as we used to by leasing our old movies to TV. I was talking to the movie library about this and I asked them what they thought the problem was. They said, "Mr. Schwerdloff, people today just can't relate to black-and-white films— they're like antiques." That's when the idea flashed in my head: modernize the black-and-whites!

For instance, in our great old Civil War movie, *Brother Against Brother*, there's the scene where Mrs. Jeffries is alone in the house, rocking, waiting to hear how Gettysburg turned out. She knows one of her sons has died but she doesn't know which one. In the original scene, Mrs. Jeffries hears a knock at the door. She goes to answer it. It is a Western Union boy with a telegram. She opens it. She says, "It's Luther," and starts to cry. The Western Union boy takes off his hat and says, "Your Luther was a fine boy, ma'am. He used to stick up for me at the schoolhouse when the other kids'd make fun of me on account of my mama's being—well, you know." Then Mrs. Jeffries goes back to her rocking chair and reads the telegram again. While she's still crying, she says, "Now Luther's sticking up for the angels."

In the modernized version, instead of a knock at the door, I had the telephone ring. Then Mrs. Jeffries walks off screen, same as she did before. Then comes the moving scene with the Western Union guy. I cut that out but kept the next scene where she reenters the room with the telegram in her hand. It was a clever way to do it because the audience figures she has written down what was told to her on the phone and now is reading it. The only drawback to this version is that the audience never finds out which son died. But that wasn't the point of the movie. The point was that it's sad when you lose a son no matter how you find out. But the phone made people relate to it more.

I decided to put in modern sounds in the background of all the old movies—garbage disposals, car crashes, airplanes taking off, Velcro ripping open. I think familiar noises relax people.

Ike loved the idea when I told it to him. He was so excited about it, he begged me to let him handle it. That Ike, say what you will about him, but there wasn't a thing I said I wanted to do that he wasn't happy to take off my hands. Unfortunately, Ike had too many things on his tray and didn't move on it. I had other things on my mind too, so it took me a while before I noticed.

One thing I wanted to take care of right away was the lack of publicity about *My Progress*. When I asked Ike about it, he told me he wasn't allowing the press on the set at all. He said it wouldn't do us any good. This was dumb. If the film was going so well, why not cash in on it?

So I made a few calls to people in the press and told them there was a good story for them in Marfa, Texas.

FROM MARILYN BECK'S COLUMN OF OCTOBER 3, 1983

FROM WUNDERKIND TO BLUNDERKIND? I've been to Texas to see the filming of hit-maker Ferris Keneally's *My Progress* and I can tell you I've never seen such chaos. All the rumors I've been printing are true: the endless delays on the set due to Keneally's newfound perfectionism; his feud with the Texas Film Board; his tempestuous love affair with his leading lady, the new French unknown Simone Bejour; his bitterness over interference by studio production chief Ike Spergyle. Looks like a MAJOR FLOP in the making. . . .

Bucky didn't see the Marilyn Beck column. He didn't see any of the bad publicity we were getting. Anytime it was necessary, I had the prop people print up fake newspapers replacing the bad publicity with good. It was necessary quite a lot of the time. It cost a lot but it was worth it.

I did however send the Marilyn Beck column, and all others like it, to Keneally. I thought they might goad him into action.

FROM IKE SPERGYLE TO FERRIS KENEALLY

October 4, 1983

Dear Ferris,

Please find enclosed article, which I hope you will find interesting.

Also enclosed is a calendar. Evidently you do not have one or you would not be forty-two days behind schedule. Knowing how busy you are, I have taken the liberty of circling our opening day, a day you specifically requested because it will allow the film to open in time for Academy Award consideration. I have also circled the last day on which you can finish shooting and still have time for editing, scoring, my comments, etc. That day is November 28.

Lastly, may I remind you that if you fail to meet the opening date, your film will be too late for Academy

Award consideration and we must forfeit our first run
theaters and scramble for anything we can get. This
would be undeserving of a project of this magnitude.

Please notify me immediately how much of the
lost time you can make up.

With warmest personal regards,

Ike Spergyle

SHOOTING REPORT

TO: Ike Spergyle   DATE: 10/7/83
FROM: Howie Perlmutter (Unit mgr.)   SUBJECT: XA573

SHOOTING DAY # __27__

No shooting done because Keneally couldn't de-
cide if his daughter would like it better if the curtains in
scene 66 were opened or closed.

But the day turned out well. I finished the sleeve
on the sweater I'm knitting and it looks really good.

The crew is also keeping busy with games and
things.

49 days behind schedule.

EDITORIAL FROM *THE MARFA MORNING CRIER*, SEPTEMBER 25, 1983

OUR RUDE VISITORS

We'll admit that we were pretty excited when Mayor
MacGruder announced that a Hollywood movie was to
be filmed in our town. Along with the rest of Marfa, we
got out our autograph books. But our film fantasy has
turned into a horror picture.

It takes a lot to test Marfa's patience. We endured the noise, the electrical blackouts, the disgraceful litter, even the inconsiderate behavior of many of the cast, none of whom, we might add, are actors we've heard of, like Julie Andrews or Cheech and Chong.

But the pranks! While it is impossible to prove that the movie people are responsible for the recent surge in obscene phone calls, we still believe it. But what we as a newspaper and as private citizens cannot allow to continue is the taking of babies from their homes without the consent of their parents, and the subsequent use of the infants for the entertainment of the crew.

Case in point: the O'Donnell twins, Timmy and Jimmy. Age: 10 months. Wednesday afternoon, during their nap, while their mother, as she tearfully recalled, "was mashing up some apples for them," members of the Hollywood crew sneaked in and "borrowed" the children and used them as hood ornaments in a race between a sound truck and an animal trailer. Predictably, one of the twins was lost.

Human loss, even if it is only a twin, and a baby twin at that, is still to be mourned. A good new beginning might be if the film crew, as a gesture of regret, would buy all 600 of the 16-inch real copper replicas of the historic Marfa Tree, which are currently on sale at Service Drug for $12.95. It is fitting that the owner of the store is Mr. Arthur O'Donnell.

The Marfa editorial was sent to Bucky by the mayor with an angry letter demanding an apology and a cessation of the pranks.

Bucky never saw the letter. I had his secretary clear all his mail through me.

FROM FRIAR CURRIE'S JOURNAL

October 8, 1983

I wish I had seen a movie before producing one. Then I would know how worried to be.

Here's the thing: I know of a surety now that we are not filming *The Pilgrim's Progress*. I know *The Pilgrim's Progress* by heart and there is no train in it.

And it makes me red hot but I think Ferris is lying to me.

I had better lay my hands on a script. Pronto.

12:02 A.M.

. . . and it was late at night, in the room where Ferris lay sleeping, that I found it, thick and heavy like a rock. And I took it. Ferris did not hear me. Hermits are very quiet. Even when we fall, people do not hear us.

It was wrong to steal the script, I know, I know, I know, I know, but I *had* to take action. I mean, come on, I am the producer. I have my rights.

. . . And it is now that I have laid down the script upon the table. And my heart is sick. If this is *The Pilgrim's Progress,* then I am King Nebuchadnezzar.

I have been a Hermit all my days on the earth and if I am going to leave the brotherhood to produce a major motion picture for Christmas of 1984, then it must be one that will help others.

What can I do? I am so confused. I shall pray.

1:27 A.M.

I have heard my instructions. I shall call Bucky. I shall tell him how everything has gone wrong, how the masterpiece we set out to create has been spoiled and how now we are working on, in Howie Perlmutter's words, "the turkey of all time."

Bucky will solve everything.

BUCKY SCHWERDLOFF

When Friar Currie called, I was working on my Movie Modernization Program. I had written a memo to Franklin Getchell, one of our special effects people, asking him if it was possible to remove the eyeglasses from everyone wearing them in all our old movies. Nobody wears glasses anymore. They wear contacts. And I thought that people wearing glasses made our movies look old-fashioned. Franklin had written back that it was possible to eliminate the glasses but it would be incredibly expensive and there would be white circles around people's eyes where the glasses had been. This was good news—my idea could be done. Then Friar Currie called.

I have to say I was shocked to hear the movie was in trouble. We'd been getting such good press! I don't mean to point fingers, but Ike should've been keeping a closer eye on the movie. Of course, ultimately I was responsible but my management style is to hire the best people possible and then turn them loose. It's not necessary for me to poke my nose in every month to find out how they're doing their jobs or even what their jobs are. Obviously Ike couldn't handle this responsibility, which, you know, was also a surprise to me since he'd come so highly recommended.

I went to his office to talk to him. I don't like to play the dictator but I had to do something. I didn't want the movie to fail.

IKE SPERGYLE

When Bucky came in my office, I braced myself. Whenever Bucky came into my office, I braced myself. I was always afraid he had a great idea. Anyway, he sat down and he said, "My Progress is in trouble." Yeah, and the South is losing the Civil War, I thought.

After he recounted what that stupid monk had told him, I said the best thing would be for me to go to Texas and try to straighten things out. Bucky kept asking me if I really thought the movie would be a failure, how big, who would be blamed, etc. Then, all of a sudden, he said, "Wait, I know! Let's get Ferris to sign something that guarantees the movie won't be a failure."

I said, "We'd never be able to hold Keneally to it." But Bucky said, "We'll get it notarized!"

Bucky left my office as Beatrice, my secretary, came in with the shooting report for that day, a report that informed me Keneally was ordering another nose job for Bejour.

In a way I was glad Bucky knew about the trouble. Now I could take some action.

10/27/83

CEASE WORK IMMEDIATELY ON THE BEJOUR NOSE. NO FURTHER ALTERATIONS MAY BE MADE WITHOUT MY APPROVAL. I WILL ARRIVE TEXAS TOMORROW 5:52 AND WILL WANT YOU AT ONCE FOR MEETING. PLEASE ARRANGE FOR ME TO SEE ALL FOOTAGE—OR, FROM THE REPORTS I'VE BEEN GETTING, ALL INCHAGE. WITH WARMEST PERSONAL REGARDS, IKE SPERGYLE.

. . .

KENEALLY IGNORED SPERGYLE'S DIRECTIVE. HE FLEW IN DR. PAUL KNABENHANS, THE COSMETIC SURGEON BEST KNOWN FOR LOWERING MUAMMAR QADDAFI'S FOREHEAD, TO DISCUSS STARTING FROM SCRATCH AND BUILDING A NEW BRIDGE FOR BEJOUR'S NOSE. SPERGYLE ARRIVED BEFORE THE WORK BEGAN. WHEN HE SAW THE NOSE, HE AGREED THAT IT WAS REPELLENT. HOWEVER, HE WOULD APPROVE ONLY REMEDIAL WORK AND NOT THE NEW CONSTRUCTION KENEALLY WANTED.

IKE SPERGYLE

I called the meeting as soon as I got to Texas. Present were Howie, Keneally, and Currie.

Howie summarized what had gone on: the destruction of sets for imperceptible details and then their rebuilding; the complete disregard for the budget, and on and on.

Keneally did not deny Howie's story. He just said that the film would be finished on time and it would be a great film.

I said this was not good enough. There was no possible way the movie could be finished on time, and from what I knew of the script, the prospect of its being a great movie were slim. I insisted that changes be made.

Keneally became humble. He asked me to have faith in him and give him the chance to finish the movie. He said it was more than a movie to him. It was his way of trying to give his life meaning. He might fail, he might fall short, but would I really deny him the chance?

I told him I was sympathetic to his desire to regain his sanity but that his first priority should be to get out the most commercial movie possible.

He said I was an insensitive, uncreative, bureaucratic cog and I should go hang myself with red tape. I told him that he was a petulant, pampered, spoiled brat. We almost got into a fistfight but Currie interrupted. He said, "There is a simple solution to all of this," and then he held up that stupid book.

156

I said, "There is a simpler solution. I'm canceling the project!"

Keneally shouted back at me, "We'll see about that!" and he picked up the phone. The next thing I know he has that idiot on the phone. He said, "Bucky, we're having a row. Only you can settle it." Then he told him about how great the movie was going to be. Then I got on the phone and told him my side, how it would surely flop and we would do best to cut our losses now.

Bucky said, "Well, I've heard both sides and I like Ferris's better!"

Ike slammed down the phone. I must say I was feeling triumphant, but then Ike said he didn't care what Bucky said. He said he was in charge and he was determined to see his wishes were met.

He presented me with a list of suggestions for the script. Now, look. This is the thing: I had never given him a script, but with his customary chicanery, he had laid his hands on one and had brought the full, puny weight of his critical powers to bear on it.

Naturally, I was not going to read his little list. I crumpled it and threw it across the room. But the friar ran over and brought it back. He said, "You must read this." Poor old friar. He thought Ike was trying to get the project back to being *The Pilgrim's Progress*. So I read the thing out loud.

SPERGYLE'S LIST OF SUGGESTIONS

1. Do not assume that the main action of your film will be sufficient to hold the attention of your audience. Never assume anything. "Assume" makes an "ass" out of "u" and "me." Therefore, use a catchy score for the people who will not be held by the story. We own rights to unreleased Diana Ross single, "Come Here and Shut the Door." Could release this as "Love Theme from *My Progress*." This gets our name all over the radio.

2. People have to be able to understand the plot of the movie whenever they come in, no matter when that is. Please adjust script accordingly.

3. During the last minute of the movie, one character must summarize to another character the action of the movie in a short and attractive sentence. This will aid audience members who would not otherwise be capable of doing so in describing the film to their friends in a manner which is beneficial to us.

FROM FRIAR CURRIE'S JOURNAL

October 29, 1983

. . . When I heard Ike's suggestions, I knew I could not count on him for help. So, look, look here, I told Ferris that he must change the script and he told me that he would not. I insisted that he must. And he insisted that he could not. And I said it was essential to my full participation in the project. And he said that there could only be one vision on the screen and that it must be his. And I said that the vision must be Mr. Bunyan's and until it was, I would go on a hunger strike. Ferris said that he did not believe me, but then I swore with my hand upon the Bible. And then I saw by the coffee that there were sugar donuts and I told Ferris that he could have fifteen minutes to think it over. When I finished the sugar donuts, Ferris told me that he could not change the script. Now I am not eating. My life is in his hands.

I'd been seeing the awful things about the movie in the papers. I was worried so I called Meelie. I read all the things to her and got her worried. She called Ike and he said that yes, the movie was having problems but he was going down to Texas to straighten things out. Meelie asked him about Bucky. Ike said he'd explained everything to him and that Bucky took it badly at first but seemed fine now.

But that night Bucky called me. I knew right away that something was wrong. It was three in the morning and Bucky usually goes to bed at eight right after *Tupper*, which is a show he likes about a turtle. He said, "I need to know something about Dad. Remember when we were seven?" He meant when he was seven. "And Dad got so upset with Ava Gardner in that Africa movie?" Bucky was talking about a movie the studio did in the fifties called *Nearer the Sun*. While they were shooting in the Congo, there was a scene where Miss Gardner had to ride on one of the elephants. But every time she got on this elephant, he coiled his trunk back so it was just practically right in front of her. Then he blew water through it and knocked her off his back. Finally Miss Gardner refused to get back on him—or any elephant—and I must say I don't blame her. Meanwhile, though, the production stopped while the director and everyone tried to coax her back up. This was costing the studio tons of money and Daddy decided to fly to the Congo and get the matter settled.

When Miss Gardner saw that Daddy had come all

that way to get her on the elephant, she got on the elephant. And the elephant behaved and they got the scene in one take*.

So I told Bucky this and Bucky said, "Thank you. Remember the wooden masks Daddy bought us?" I said I did and he said, "They were nice," and then he said, "Good night!"

---

1. Couldn't we grow our own vegetables for the commissary to save money? We could use that field on lot 3 by the lake. Plus, we could get stars to come and plant. Then they'll want to do their movies here so they can see how their vegetables are doing.

2. For Movie Modernization Program: how come all the young people in old movies look old? I think it's because of those baggy pants. Is it possible to do something so that they are wearing jeans? Also, is there any way to get Laurence Olivier a haircut in *Fletcher Jones*?

3. Make reservations to go to Texas. Be sure to bring my big book of Scramblets for the flight.

5. Let's have a sign made for the new garden: "Victory Garden." This year is our year to start winning again!

---

*A classic Hollywood joke arose out of this incident: When the elephant saw that Schwerdloff had come to Africa, the elephant jumped up, grabbed Ava Gardner out of her tent, put her on his back, gave her a little kiss, saluted Schwerdloff, and said, "Ready when you are!" Schwerdloff said to the director, Howard Hawks, "How come all of a sudden the elephant's being so nice?" Howard Hawks said, "We told him you were Harry Cohn!"

CHAPTER 9

BUCKY TO THE RESCUE

BUCKY SCHWERDLOFF

In a way the crisis with the movie was my fault. I had been far away from the production and my mind was thinking about other matters. I had given Ferris too free a hand.

Now I'm an idea man. I'm good at suggestions. So I bought myself a chair for the set and I had them put HEAD OF THE STUDIO on it and I rolled up my sleeves. I was ready to give it my 100 percent.

. . .

THIS CARD ACCOMPANIED A GIFT OF AN ANTIQUE TOY TRAIN PRESENTED TO KENEALLY BY SCHWERDLOFF UPON HIS ARRIVAL IN MARFA, TEXAS:

November 5, 1983

Dear Ferris,

Let me say "I'm sorry" as I should have a long time ago for not having been here before when you needed me. I'll be there tomorrow and every day right by your side. For as long as it takes.

Good luck!

Bucky

SHOOTING REPORT

TO: *Ike Spergyle*   DATE: *11/6/83*
FROM: *Howie Perlmutter (Unit mgr.)*   SUBJECT: *XA573*

SHOOTING DAY # __44__

Shooting began late due to Bucky's arrival on set. Keneally introduced him to cast and Schwerdloff asked if he might say a few words. He said he hoped people would not be made nervous by his presence and that he was not here to look over anyone's shoulder. He was here to support everyone and he had the greatest faith in the cast and in *My Progress* and in Keneally. What is he—a nut?

Shooting began at 10:00. The scene to be shot was the scene where Terrence is walking down the corridor of the train and he opens a door and sees himself as a boy sitting between his parents. The boy is crying, his parents are laughing.

163

Just as Chapman Dorn* reached the compartment door, Schwerdloff shouted, "Wait! I have a great idea!" Then he told Keneally his idea. Keneally refused to use the idea. When Schwerdloff pressed him, Keneally walked off the set.

Crew dismissed at 10:10

*Chapman Dorn played Terrence.

BUCKY SCHWERDLOFF

I just thought it would have been funny if on the train of Ferris's life, two fat people with drinks and food in their hands tried to pass each other in one of those narrow hallways.

Ferris said no, absolutely not, but some of the cast that was around heard it and they laughed. I still think it was a mistake not using it. That movie could've used a little humor.

SHOOTING REPORT

TO: *Ike Spergyle*   DATE: *11/15/83*
FROM: *Howie Perlmutter (Unit Mgr.)*   SUBJECT: *XA573*

SHOOTING DAY # ___53___

. . . Another argument between Bucky and Keneally. Keneally refused another suggestion as he has all Schwerdloff's suggestions. Tension high.

SHOOTING REPORT
───────────────────────────

TO: *Ike Spergyle*   DATE: *12/02/83*
FROM: *Howie Perlmutter (Unit mgr.)* SUBJECT: *XA573*

SHOOTING DAY # __73__

Shot scene 101. This shows Terrence as a boy, lazing in the sunshine for 25 minutes. Real time. At the end of shooting, Keneally wept uncontrollably. I thought he might be going crazy again but then he explained that he had never been allowed 25 minutes real time as a child.

I wasn't able to finish the collar on my sweater today because I wanted to watch a fight between Bucky and Keneally. Should finish tomorrow. Will let you know.

BUCKY SCHWERDLOFF

Ferris just refused all help. There I was, right by his side, making suggestion after suggestion—for a movie, I might add, I did not even understand—and he didn't take one of them. It could be the greatest idea in the world and if it didn't come from him, he didn't want it.

I don't know if I told you this, but I had a great idea for a way to get a lot of people to go to the movie. I know a lot of people watch TV instead of going to the movies, so I thought why not make the movies more like TV? Why not put commercials in them?

Not only that, I knew exactly what the commercials should be. Progresso Soups. I figured Terrence would look out the window of the train and say, *"My Progress!"* Then the porter would put a bowl of soup in front of him and Terrence would say, "My Progresso!"

When I told this idea to Ferris, he put his hands over his ears and started singing, "La-la-la-la-la-la-la!" At the time, he just wasn't big enough to use other people's ideas. Ordinarily I would have made him use my ideas, but you hate to push the mentally ill.

I just could never convince Ferris we were on the same team.

. . .

BUCKY SCHWERDLOFF'S PRESENCE IN MARFA COMPOUNDED THE PRESSURES ON KENEALLY. IKE SPERGYLE CONTINUED TO PUSH KENEALLY TO COMPLETE THE FILM AS SOON AS POSSIBLE. IN A LETTER DATED

DECEMBER 18, 1983, HE WROTE KENEALLY, "AS YOU KNOW, YOUR FILM IS UNBELIEVABLY OVERSCHEDULE. ONCE BEFORE I SENT YOU A CALENDAR WITH KEY DATES CIRCLED. I THOUGHT THIS WOULD BE A USEFUL GUIDE FOR PLANNING YOUR SCHEDULE. AS YOU RETURNED THE CALENDAR TO THIS OFFICE SHREDDED, I WILL NOT TROUBLE TO EXTEND SUCH A KINDNESS AGAIN. . . .

KENEALLY TURNED INCREASINGLY TO SIMONE BEJOUR FOR SOLACE. THE FOLLOWING LETTERS WERE WRITTEN TO MS. BEJOUR WHILE SHE WAS IN THE MARFA MEMORIAL HOSPITAL FOR HER FOURTH NOSE JOB UNDER THE CARE OF DR. KNABENHANS.

FROM FERRIS KENEALLY TO SIMONE BEJOUR

Marfa, Texas
December 4, 1983

Simone, my darling,

Please do not think that because I have made you have four nose jobs I do not love you just the way you are. You are the most blessed thing that has ever happened to me, the one silver light in the black tunnel of this movie. I spend my days in thanks that I have found you.

Your own,

F.

December 5, 1983

Dear,

Every day it gets worse. You cannot know—the way everyone here is ganging—that wretched Ike is here, snipping and picking and harping and whining and

168

threatening and screaming and pushing and nagging and coughing and shoving letters under my door and— wait. There's the phone. Ringing and clanging and calling and shrieking for me to answer it—oh, no. It wasn't the phone.

Did I tell you? I must. Bucky is, Bucky is, Bucky is here, and, oh God, oh, God. The friar turns out to be a bodyguard for John Bunyan and has gone on a hunger strike until I reinsert all the words he misses. I think I can stop this: I sent some tarts to his room. I'm not really upset with him. He's . . . he's a good fellow. But—oh! This has been—People certainly don't treat the insane the way they used to.

But mostly it's the time away from you that makes this all so hard to bear. I wish there were more roses in Marfa to send you.

F.

FROM SIMONE BEJOUR TO FERRIS KENEALLY

December 5, 1983

Chérie,

It is just a few hours before they start up on my nose again. I will try my hardest to have it be right for you. I would let them do anything to my nose as long as through it I could breathe. For if I could not breathe, I could not be with you—at least the way I want to.

Loving you,

Simone

December 6, 1983

Dear,

Today Bucky was nagging me to make the characters more "real." He says none of the characters ever says, "See you later!" Friar Currie said that if anyone in the movie says, "See you later!" he will refuse all liquids. It is so—oh, God.

Wait. Never mind. No wait. How is everyone getting the script? I've tried—*no*. I *have*, I *have* been good about keeping the script secret. I *have*! Even the cast only gets the pages they're in that day. I didn't—I was so good about not letting Ike have one and somehow he got one. How? How could he have? Now he gave one to Bucky and the friar. Who else has one? Who? (Pauline Kael? If Pauline Kael has one, I'm dead.)

As I am writing this to you, I am in your room. You are under sedation. Your face is wrapped in bandages, which reminds me of what a gift you are to me.

Love and love again,

F.

December 7, 1983

Darling,

Welcome home! It's been so hard without you. The Texas Film people are nagging me—hound me, they hound me day and night. The friar hasn't eaten in a week, and worst of all—that hideous Ike.

But despite all that, I woke up today becalmed,

170

because you are coming home from the hospital to be with me. I love you so much.

We are filming late tonight in the moonlight, so don't wait up for me. I will wake you with my kisses and

All my love,

F.

FERRIS KENEALLY

The night we were supposed to shoot the scene where Terrence visits his grave, it was cloudy. We lost the moon, so I postponed shooting. Though we were, if I recall correctly, a bit behind schedule, I wasn't troubled because, you see, it was Simone's first night home from the hospital and I was longing to be with her. On the way to the motel, I stopped at the liquor shop and had the fellows there wrap me up a bottle of champagne, which they do by tying a bunch of balloons on top—very festive.

Standing outside the door to our room, I thought of Simone's nose—what if I didn't like it? Dr. Knabenhans had called me that morning to say he thought it his best work. Remembering that, I said to myself, "It *will* be beautiful."

When I opened the door and looked at Simone, however, it was rather difficult to assess the work as there was a gross-looking man on top of her, impeding my view. There was something, I don't know, vaguely familiar about the fellow, but I thought I might be confusing him with a warthog I had seen on the local news which had lost its hair in a cancer treatment.

Seeing me, Simone screamed. The man's head jerked up, flooding the mirror behind the bed with the vile features of his face. I stared at him, barely able to believe it. Outside of my mother, this was the last person in the world I wanted to find in bed with Simone. It was Ike Spergyle.

172

CHAPTER 10

"CUT!"

FERRIS KENEALLY

I was stunned past all imagining. Ike Spergyle in bed with Simone!

Before I could collect my thoughts, Ike yelled, "Goddammit, Ferris, you're supposed to be shooting! Don't tell me you're behind schedule again!" My thoughts, however, were far from the film. I was thinking only of Simone having an affair with Ike. I said, "Just tell me—how long?"

Simone said, "Five more minutes?" That's not what I meant but I couldn't even talk. Suddenly I saw it all: how Ike got the script, why Simone kept changing the wedding plans—oh, the wedding! Here's the—Oh, listen to the thing about the wedding: first it was to be a church wedding, then a simple ceremony at the justice of the peace's, then—and this, I was a fool, this really should've tipped me off—then she wanted to get married in the desert, without witnesses, without words, without rings, just the two of us, not facing each other, thinking our vows.

Good Christ, I felt so ridiculous bursting through the door, that champagne in my hand and that humiliating look on my face that showed not only my joy at her homecoming, but also the longing I had for her to be happy that I was home. The saddest thing was that Dr. Knabenhans was right. Simone's nose was perfect. And now it was Ike's.

For a minute—it seemed like an hour—I couldn't do anything. I couldn't move, I couldn't speak. I wanted to move my hands to close the door, but I couldn't even do that.

IKE SPERGYLE

I deny any relationship I have had with Simone Bejour. I am a happily married man.

I fell in love with Ike on the second I learned that his approval was necessary before Ferris could give me that part. Still but I loved Ferris because Ike, he could not give me the part without the approval of Ferris. It was the classic situation: I was torn between two lovers. Always Ike tells me Ferris could not love me so much as he says he did because of what he does to my nose. At the time, I does not mind all the nose operations because the studio pays for everything and always I could persuade the doctors to do little extra things such as, you know, scrape my teeth. Also, when you're in the hospital like that, they shampoo your hair for you, which is very nice, very old-world.

Anyhow, when Ferris opens the door, the first thing that comes to me is, "Oh, my God! He's discovered us! He's going to kill us!" But then in a voice very hoarse I can't barely even hear him, he asked us how much more time we need. Then for such a long time he says nothing.

Finalement, Ike said, "Ferris, would you mind closing the door?" Ike was bothered, I think, by a family in the hall who are watching us. Ike has that prudish American morality about his nudity. He was ashamed with his body and I can see why.

But Ferris, he does not move. It was as if he did not hear Ike. So Ike, he himself gets up to close the door and the second he touches the doorknob, quick as a cat, Ferris grabs the throat of Ike and he says in a very low voice, "You'll regret this. I'm going to Bucky."

Oooh, I loved to hear Ferris speak in this way—so low and growly! I really wanted to make love with him right on that second but before I could say this thing to him, he leaves.

BUCKY SCHWERDLOFF

I was sound asleep and I heard this pounding on the door. I opened it and Ferris was standing there with a bottle of champagne and a bunch of balloons that said, "I LOVE YOU!" Obviously he was trying to make up for being so mean to me on the set. He said, "Bucky, I've got to talk to you."

I said, "You don't have to say anything, Ferris. The balloons say it all."

I guess I embarrassed him because he changed the subject. He said, "Bucky, we've got to talk about the movie. I'm not going to be able to finish it."

I said, "But why?"

He said, "It's Ike. I can't work with him here. He's distracting me from my work. He's not creative like you are, Bucky."

I said, "Yes, Ferris, I know. But he's very good at something. That's why we hired him."

And he said, "Bucky, he's been having an affair with Simone."

I said, "He couldn't be. He's married!" But Ferris had seen them. He said he was leaving to fly back to L.A.

That was it. If he left Texas, there went our blockbuster. There went the studio. There went my reputation. Ferris had to stay. I said, "Please, Ferris. Don't go. Don't quit. You can't quit. You're making such a great movie!"

Ferris said, "I don't know, I don't know—" He said he had always figured he could make a masterpiece of a movie if he only tried, but now he was trying and this was definitely not a masterpiece. He said, "Maybe slop is all I can do."

I couldn't believe that the man who made *Boogaloo* was talking this way. I said, "Ferris, you are the greatest director of all time. You just need to remember, like they say in *The Little Engine That Could,* you can do anything you put your mind to."

Ferris said, "Not with Ike here I can't."

And I said, "I'll send him back to Hollywood on the next plane."

He said, "And can you do something about the friar?"

I said, "I'll speak to him right away. How about it, Ferris? Will you make the movie now?"

Ferris said, "I don't know. It's just . . . Simone. How can I face her every day?"

And I said, "Well, that's easy. You told me once you hoped your film would help you get over your heartaches. Why don't you use it now to help you get over Simone?"

I was glad I thought of this. Ferris broke into a huge grin and he said, "Bucky, you're one in a million." Then he shot the cork out of the bottle and we drank champagne.

I was glad to have that settled. I gave Ferris a week off to go back to Hollywood and make some changes he wanted in the script. Since I was up, I decided to go ahead and settle the Friar Currie problem. I called him and asked him to come by.

I got right to the point. I said, "Friar, I was talking to Ferris. He's going to be taking a few days off to rewrite the script. But I'm sorry to tell you that he is not going to be changing it back to *The Pilgrim's Progress.* I know this is disappointing to you, but you have to admit that no one but you likes that thing—"

The friar cut me off before I could finish. He said, "You must insist. Are you not his boss?" I said, "Yes, but I think Ferris is going to bring us a great movie."

The friar said, "But if it does not say what we believe in—" Now by this point I was getting a little mad. I'm usually not the type to lose my temper but I was tired and

179

he was being such a pest. So I said, "I believe in Ferris. And you should too." And Friar Currie said he wanted to make a movie that would give people hope. But that wasn't what Ferris wanted, he said. He said, "Ferris cares only about himself, and because of that his movie—your movie—will be a failure as big as the mountains!"

I said, "Don't say that, Friar, please!"

And he said, "I must say it if it is true!"

I said, "No, Friar, here is what you have to do. You have to get on the team!" Then I said, "Friar, I hate to criticize you, but you obviously have trouble admitting it when you're in the wrong. Now we are not all here to make a movie just for you. We are here to make a movie that millions of people will love and remember. Therefore, we are going ahead with Ferris's movie, not yours. And my decision is *final*. Furthermore, you will end your hunger strike or I will have to fire you. Now, good night."

I don't think I've ever had to be so hard on one of my employees, but he just wouldn't give up. Plus, I have to admit, his remark about "a failure as big as the mountains" really rubbed me the wrong way. I hate that kind of talk. I really hate it.

FROM FRIAR CURRIE'S JOURNAL

December 7, 1983

In the movie business I have learned you have to take the bad with the bad. Bucky told me tonight that it is definite: Ferris will not film *The Pilgrim's Progress*. And Bucky expected that I would take this heartbreaking news and be meek. Yeah right. The meek may inherit the earth but I notice they do not get too many movies made. I have had it up to here with not getting this movie made.

I prayed to God for direction. And a vision came

before me. I saw Flann Washburn and the Communitarians in the town of New Salvage, Wisconsin. And the Communitarians had sent forth invitations to the townspeople to join them for an All Faiths Supper. But on the night of the supper, hoodlums from the town snuck into the sacristy and added great quantities of pepper to the Holy Dirt.

That night at the supper, the Communitarians sprinkled the dirt over their food and gave the blessing, "Whence all food came, whence all life." But when they ate of the food, the Communitarians sneezed and gasped and fanned their mouths, calling for water. Now the townspeople laughed until they fell from their seats.

And that night Flann Washburn said, "I don't know about you but I've had enough. We shall not be taken advantage of again." Washburn's words rallied the Communitarians. It was then that they decided to abandon their goal of working with others and now to rely only upon themselves; this was the birth of the Hermits of Christ.*

God sent me this vision for a reason. When I opened my eyes and looked out the window, the moon appeared from behind thick clouds and cast its heavenly light on the movie trucks in the field below.

Now I know what I must do. I must not be taken advantage of any longer. I must not listen to Bucky. I must film *The Pilgrim's Progress* myself while Ferris is away this week.

*The Hermits did not leave the cruelty of New Salvage unavenged. That night, before leaving town, Flann Washburn and his followers gathered gum from the trees and plugged up the udders of all the cows in town. New Salvage, once a thriving cheese town, soon went bankrupt, after a brief success as a steak center.

December 8, 1983

I have just brought to an end my first day of shooting.
We shot in the field behind Texas Burger. I am using
Ferris's actors. I told them Ferris had asked me to
film some scenes while he was away. One of the
actors became suspicious because in Ferris's movie he
was playing a crippled man and now he was playing
Mr. Quickfeet. Many of the actors also became suspicious so I explained to them that, okay, in truth, this
was an extra movie. Now there were many protests and
the actors said they would call the union. I told them I
would pay them double overtime and that shut them
up.

Double overtime is costly, but no amount of money
is too much to visualize properly Mr. Bunyan's book.
Also, I can bury it in the budget for Ferris's movie. I
had to pay Howie Perlmutter a large sum of money to
keep his big trap shut to Ferris. I found a way to bury
that too. It is necessary to grease a lot of palms out
here, I have noticed.

December 15, 1983

And tonight we finished the movie. Hot dog! The last
scene where Christian awakes and finds that it was
all but a dream occurred well. Miss Spencer, who
played Christian's mate, was not as good as everyone
else. I fear she has no presence. I would not use her
again.

When I get back to Hollywood, I shall have to
learn what to do with the movie. It is hard to know
when I will get back to Hollywood because it is taking
Ferris so long to finish his film. Me: 7 days. Ferris: 73
days and still going.

I hope God will forgive me for mocking Ferris this

way, but even God must be getting a little tired of Ferris's movie, although I know God cannot get tired.

As I came back from wrapping the film, I saw Ferris, who had just returned. He said, "Friar, I know you had different ideas about how everything would go here. I hope you're not too upset with how it's turned out."

And I said, "I had time to think about it this week. And I no longer think you should film *The Pilgrim's Progress.*"

And he said, "You're a jolly good sport, Friar."

Now I hoped so, too, would he be when my film came out.

I was so very worried about myself when Ferris caught Ike and me. Before he went away, the affair, I begged him not to hold it against me and please to keep me in the movie. He said our affair was in the past but still very much he wanted me for the movie.

Then when he is away, he is sending flowers to my room with little cards that say, "Can't wait to work with you again." I did to wonder if still he was not having the interested feeling in me, so when he gets back, I make the advance to him so I could secure my position in a way that a contract never could, you know, but he rebuffed me.

After Ferris took Ike's and my affair so very bad, Ike and I decided to end. It is always hard, yes, to end—you have so many private, close-to-the-heart things—but in our case, it was more easy since not one of either of us had the feelings for each other. At the start, I wanted favors and does not want to give Ike sex. Ike only wanted sex and does not want to give me favors. So, we compromised. I gave him sex, he gave me favors. You know, vraiment, they are right. Compromise is the only thing that makes a relationship work.

Anyhow, the night before we start to shoot again, Ferris, he was so eager to start again, so very excited. Before, when Ferris was first filming us in the movie, he was very grim, nearly in anguish. But that night, I saw him in the dining room and he was laughing and waving to people and clapping his hands. Once, for a second, he did a little dance.

The next morning, Ferris sent me a note to my dressing trailer that said, "I wouldn't have anyone play this part but you." With it, he sent an enormous chocolate heart. There was a knife stuck in the center, which, at the time, I thought was to help me cut it. Looking back, I would say it was a sign, yes?

SHOOTING REPORT

TO: Ike Spergyle   DATE: 12/16/83
FROM: Howie Perlmutter (Unit mgr.)   SUBJECT: XA573

SHOOTING DAY # ___81___

Wait till you hear this: shooting began on schedule. I'm not kidding. Keneally even arrived early to check details.

Then shot the scene where Bejour is dragged several hundred feet through the mud. After 8 takes, Keneally asked to try it with "more rocks." The additional rocks created the effect Keneally was after and he ordered a print. We had time to shoot tomorrow's scenes where Bejour falls off a horse and then a cow steps on her head. Keneally was able to get this, a very difficult stunt for which Bejour has no training, in only 15 takes!

Only one delay. Bucky wanted an idea of his put in and Keneally refused.

TO: Ike Spergyle   *DATE: 12/22/83*
FROM: Howie Perlmutter (Unit mgr.)   *SUBJECT: XA573*

SHOOTING DAY # ___87___

Had to do retakes of scene 103. Yoke had not been tight enough around Bejour's neck and looked to Keneally as if it were easy to pull up the slope. Adjusted harness until Bejour's veins showed. (Did perfect take but Bejour's makeup went bad so had to reshoot.)

Then began shooting scene 116 but interrupted when Bucky yelled, "Cut!" Keneally marched over to Bucky. "Don't you ever interrupt shooting again!" he yelled. "*I* am the director!"

"But, Ferris," Schwerdloff said, "I've got a great idea!"

Keneally, struggling to control himself, said, "Bucky, please sit down."

But Bucky said, "Not now, Ferris. I think even you are going to like this idea. I meant to tell you this before we started. I saw a great *Dick Van Dyke* last night where Laura gets her toe stuck in a bowling ball. Any way we can use that?"

Keneally clenched his jaw and said, "No." Then he walked back to his chair and began talking to the cameraman.

Schwerdloff immediately turned around and began speaking with some guests he had with him on the set. Just as Keneally said, "All right, let's try it again," Schwerdloff said, "Hold it, Ferris! We've decided you're wrong and I'm right."

You should've seen the look Keneally gave him. He narrowed his eyes and said, "What do you mean 'we'?"

Schwerdloff explained that he had grown worried about Ferris's judgment. So he had found four people from Marfa whom he believed were representative of a movie audience and asked them to watch the filming and give Keneally advice on what the public likes to see. They agreed with Schwerdloff that getting things stuck on your toes was the funniest thing going.

Keneally said, "Whoever you are, the four of you, get off my set." Whoever they were, the four of them, looked at Schwerdloff to see what to do. So immediately Keneally walked up to one of the men in the group, took a big Magic Marker and drew an X across his face. Whoever they were, the four of them, left.

Then, get this, Schwerdloff, who was so mad he was red, wouldn't even look at Keneally. He sat in his chair, began yanking his hair and kicking the camera!

Keneally went over to him and said, "Get up!" Schwerdloff got up. Keneally then picked up Schwerdloff's chair and carried it to the door. He opened the door and—wait till you hear this—threw the chair outside! Then he said to Schwerdloff, "Leave this set immediately and don't come back. Or I quit!"

Shot scene 116.

I couldn't believe how rude Ferris was to my guests. I'm sorry to say, I . . . well, I lost my temper. He was stomping off and I called out to him to stop but he didn't, so I picked up a chair and threw it. He came back later and apologized.

I decided the best thing would be if I didn't come to the set anymore. Ferris just couldn't work whenever I was around. Obviously he felt inferior.

It was just as well. I had a lot of work to do on my Movie Modernization Program.

JULIA SCHWERDLOFF BUSH

Right about that time, I went to see Bucky in Marfa. Despite how positive he sounded whenever I talked to him on the phone, I was really worried. He didn't seem like his old self. I even asked him if anything was wrong, but he always told me that everything was great. He seemed so distracted, though. For my daughter's christening, he sent her steak knives. That was sweet, but . . . well, I shouldn't criticize. I'm sure someday she will eat steak and will be glad to have something to cut it with.

So I flew down. Bucky drove me to the motel and showed me his director's chair with HEAD OF THE STUDIO on it. It was outside his room. He was not allowed on the set anymore. Hearing how thoroughly he had been excluded from the production and seeing his poor little chair on the cracked pavement miles from the filming made me so sad for him.

There wasn't much to do in Marfa. He showed me how he could jump off the diving board drinking a Coke and how he'd learned to cook a version of coq au vin in his hot pot.

After we'd gone to bed, I was woken by a strange sound. It sounded like someone was being choked. I looked over at Bucky. He was sitting up, gasping for air. I asked him what was wrong but he said, "Nothing—everything's great." Then he said he was hot and wanted to sit outside for a second and get some air.

The next morning when I woke up, he was still outside in his chair. I went out and asked him what was wrong. He said, "If I did so well with Straight Rope and Squash-and-Drive, why is everything going wrong with this?"

I didn't know what to say. I just thought, *Please let this movie be finished soon and, please, please, God, let it be good.*

SHOOTING REPORT

TO: *Ike Spergyle*   DATE: *1/27/84*
FROM: *Howie Perlmutter (Unit mgr.)*   SUBJECT: *XA573*

SHOOTING DAY #   127

Last day of shooting.

Keneally finally got the shot he wanted of Terrence releasing the dove from its cage.

My sweater's finished. But this is not an end. It's a beginning. After the wrap party, I'm going to start an afghan.

IKE SPERGYLE

Bucky called when the filming finished. He was very relieved, as was I. "Bring it home," I said, "and let's see what our $51 million bought us."

FERRIS KENEALLY

We were having a dandy little wrap party on the set. Everyone was in high spirits. The press was there. We were notoriously overschedule by that point and our finishing was something of an event.

We were giving toasts when I noticed that Bucky wasn't with us. This was my fault, of course, and truthfully, I felt bad. He should be there for this, after all.

So I drove over to the motel to get him. When I walked by the window, I saw he was on the floor playing jacks. I knocked on the door. He said, "Who is it?"

I said, "It's Ferris," and he said, "Just a minute!" Then he said, "Come in," and when I did, he was sitting on his bed, talking on the phone. He said, "Okay, then, draw up the contracts, I'll talk to you later." I thought, *There's a sad thing!* Clear as a yodel, I could hear the lady on the other end doing her bit about an extension being off the hook.

When Bucky hung up, he said, "Sorry. I've just been so busy with my business affairs." Poor fellow!

I said, "If you have a moment to spare, perhaps you could come to the wrap party. Everyone's asking for you." I knew Bucky's feelings had been hurt and I expected to have to persuade him. But Bucky was a man who bore no grudges. He bounced off his bed and said, "Let's go!"

When we got to the party, I had instructed some of the crew to be waiting at the door and to hoist Bucky over their shoulders and carry him into the party. Everyone sang, "For He's a Jolly Good Fellow!" when they saw him and Bucky seemed quite appreciative.

I was feeling quite happy, quite happy that it was all over. I was even feeling rather forgiving of that shrew. I felt our scores were settled now. Then Howie Perlmutter came over and said there was something I ought to hear.

It was Simone. She had shoved herself in front of a group of reporters and was carrying on about how "cruel" I had been to her, how I had used my position to force her to do degrading things, and that I may have done physical harm to her, all because of my jealous rage over her innocent friendship with Ike Spergyle.

Naturally, I was shocked and furious at these charges. I felt then, as I feel now, that at no time did I abuse Simone. I used her as the role required. She could have quit the film at any time. But she is a monstrously ambitious woman who wanted nothing so much as to appear in a Keneally film. As for her endless complaints about what I "made" her do to her nose, let me say this. I did not like her nose. I was angry with her nose. Her nose was ruining my movie. So, I acted to make it a better nose. That was a forward—I took a forward step. The question should not be, "Why did I make Simone have four nose jobs in twelve weeks," but rather, "Why is Simone so insecure about change?"

I left the party and went straight to my room. After I did my anger exercises, I asked myself some questions: What motivated Simone to do what she had done? What steps could I take to live with what she had done? And, in the end, did her statements really affect my life? I answered these questions and felt at peace.

I went outside and saw the moon stretching its silver arms across the Texas sky. The last stragglers were wandering back from the party. I smelled the air. It was sweet with the smell of evening. I realized I would miss little Marfa. Then I went over to Simone's room, tied her to the bed, and lit the room on fire.

I felt much better. Therapy really can help you if you're willing to let it.

BUCKY SCHWERDLOFF

I'll admit that I was a little drunk. I got feeling sentimental and I wanted to be with Ferris. So I went over to the motel. There were fire trucks everywhere. I found this note on my bed:

> Do not try to contact me. I have left Texas and have the film with me. Be up front with theater owners about the iffiness of an opening date. I will be editing the film and who knows how long this will take. Love to you, my one true friend—

Ferris

CHAPTER 11

BACK IN HOLLYWOOD

FROM *VARIETY*, MARCH 10, 1984

KENEALLY IGNITES FEMME LEAD & FLEES WITH PIC;
$50 MILLION AT STAKE FOR MR. S.

Hollywood—According to sources at the Mr. S. Studio, the long-awaited Ferris Keneally feature slated for summer opening may not be seen at all. Helmsman Keneally, whose nonstop mental problems were highly publicized during the film's rocky production, has disappeared, taking all footage with him. Production chief Ike Spergyle and studio head Bucky Schwerdloff refused to comment, but an unnamed source at the studio said, "And everything that is bad is in *My Progress*. And this so came to pass because the people in charge at this place wouldn't know a good movie if one got up and bit them."

It is also rumored that Keneally tried to nix the film's leading lady, Simone Bejour, by lighting her motel room on fire while she was in it. Bejour, who claims that Keneally tied her to her bed before setting the room on fire, managed to escape the fire without being burned and suffered only a broken nose when she fell over a fire hose on her way out of the room. . . .

BUCKY SCHWERDLOFF

I don't think I've ever seen Ike so red hot as the day the *Variety* article came out. I could hear him screaming all the way from my office. At first I thought he was mad about his grain drink—Ike used to get mad at his secretary if she didn't put enough millet in. But when I went down, I saw he was yelling at Friar Currie and he was really—I mean he was practically screaming into Currie's face.

I said, "What's the matter?" and Ike said, "Nothing," but Currie said that Ike was yelling at him because the friar told a reporter from *Variety* some stuff about *My Progress*.

I tried to calm Ike down but he said, "The friar is working *against* us! We've got to fire him."

I said what was important was that we found Ferris and that we had a movie.

That's when Friar Currie said, "We have a movie."

I couldn't believe it. I said, "Well, come on! Let's roll it! When did Ferris give it to you?"

But the friar said, "Ferris had nothing to do with this film."

This didn't sound quite right. I said, "Well, where did it come from?"

He said, "I made it myself."

January 29, 1984

One thing I have learned out here: life never stops throwing things at you.

This afternoon, I walked to the screening room to see how Bucky and Ike liked my movie. And there came forth from the place laughter of such loudness I could hear it through the door which was shut. It was the laughter of Bucky and Ike.

And I heard what they were saying, things of exceeding harshness. Ike said it was the biggest waste of people since the Vietnam war. Now a mighty rush of emotion came upon me. I have tried so hard in this new world and have gotten nowhere.

But let's be frank. Is this really the world I want to get anywhere in? I think not. I can see why Flann Washburn disavowed his *Creed of the Communitarians* and chose as the watchword of our Hermit home, "Abandon Hope All Ye Who Leave Here." I remember when I talked to Father Abbot about leaving. He told me the story of Flann Washburn's death. In 1883, the Mexican outlaw Pedro Romero and his gang attacked the monastery. The Hermits were warned of the attack in time to take refuge in town. As the Hermits fled, Washburn called unto them in anger, "What kind of Hermits are you?" When one of them answered. "Come quickly! Surely Pedro Romero will take your life," Flann Washburn replied, "I don't care what he takes—I hate it out there!" Eighty bullets through his heart, Flann Washburn died a true Hermit.

For a long time I could not understand why Flann Washburn refused to leave. But now, eighty bullets— big deal! Eighty bullets seems like nothing compared to Bucky and Ferris and Ike. I shall return to my brothers.

Yet I realize my time has not been for naught. I have my movie. I shall take it back to the monastery where I know my brothers will appreciate it.

Yet I knew that the monastery does not have a projector. So I went to Supplies, hard by the commissary, and asked Mr. Trimble for one. But then Mr. Trimble asked me for the Projector Request Form which is a form Ike must sign before a projector can be released. And I said I had forgotten it and that I would go fetch it. And I walked outside and I thought to myself that I was of a certainty dead now. Then I heard a voice (God's? an angel's? Mr. Bunyan's?), and the voice said to me, "Forge it!"

And I did and now I have a projector on which to show my movie to my brothers.

Shortly after Friar Currie left, it started to rain. That afternoon, I got a call from props asking me if I would approve the construction of an ark large enough for all studio personnel. Apparently Bucky thought God was punishing us with the rain for our treatment of Friar Currie and wanted to be prepared.

Bucky was upset about that and, of course, he was tremendously upset about Keneally. Every day, more and more, it was finding Keneally that consumed him.

One night he called me at home. He said, "Maybe if we went out and looked for him?"

I said I didn't think that would help—Keneally could be anywhere in the world—but Bucky pleaded. The next thing I knew I was driving though L.A. with Bucky leaning out the window. Whenever he saw someone who he thought might be Keneally, he would tell me to slow down and he'd call out, "Ferris?" But it wouldn't be Keneally and we would drive some more. We drove all night. He wanted me to do it again the next night but I was exhausted. I later learned he went out looking with his chauffeur every night that week.

Three days before the premiere, there was still no Keneally. I was having my breakfast and the TV was on. I heard a familiar voice. Bucky.

He was holding up a picture of Keneally and looking into the camera. I can remember his words as if it were yesterday. He said, "So, if you find Ferris, or our movie, please call either me or my aide Ike Spergyle. If you can't

199

remember our number, check the back of any carton of milk." I looked at the back of our milk carton and was sickened to see Keneally's picture. Underneath it, in big red letters it said MISSING. Then, below that, it said ANY INFO CALL IKE SPERGYLE.

This was too humiliating. I wanted out. Furthermore, I dreaded the premiere more than anything: either Keneally and his film wouldn't be there or Keneally and his film would be there. It was a lose/lose situation.

So, as soon as I got to the studio, I went to Bucky's office to tell him I was resigning. As I opened his door and saw him sitting so sadly at his desk, I realized how badly he was going to take this—Keneally had quit the team and Currie had quit the team and now I was quitting the team and, not counting Bucky, that pretty well took care of the team. So without thinking—before I even realized what I was saying, I said, "Bucky, great news! Keneally saw you on TV this morning. He just called to say he's got the film ready! He says it's the best thing he's ever done!"

Bucky lit up—in one second years came off his face.

Then I said, "He'll meet you at the premiere with the movie, so everything's all set. You don't really need me anymore—my job is done. I'm going to resign because I want all the credit for this film to go to you."

Bucky said he was sorry to accept my resignation, but I could see he was happy, too. Bucky loves credit.

JULIA SCHWERDLOFF BUSH

Of course, we were coming for the premiere. Meelie and I were going to fly out the day of the premiere and spend that night and the next day with Bucky. When I called Bucky to check up on the arrangements, he sounded very up. He said, "Everything's really great. We found Ferris, he has the film all edited, Ike quit, I got a new watch-band. . . ." Ike quit! I can still feel the knife in my heart when I heard those words. "He wants the Schwerdloff name to be the only name you think of when you think of *My Progress*."

That pansy, Spergyle! We shelled out $400,000 a year for him to look after Buck. That's—what?—88,000 times better than what a baby-sitter makes—and baby-sitters don't leave the kid in the house if a fire breaks out! Actually, I'd have loved it if he'd left Buck in a fire.

The next day on the flight, I tried to calm down, but the more I thought about it, the more steamed up I got. Then, when we got off the plane, who should I see slinking along but Spergyle.

So, I yelled, "Freeze!" I marched over and pinned him against the flight insurance machine. I asked him what he was doing here.

He said, "I'm going to Nepal for a year—"

I said, "We had an agreement—"

He said, "I know, but I couldn't take your brother one second longer." Then he broke down.

My heart went out to him. I'd forgotten how much we were inflicting on him. I apologized and wished him well in Nepal. I even offered to send him the reviews. But he turned white and said, "There won't be any reviews."

I puffed up like an idiot and said, "Oh, yes, there will be. Buck found Keneally and he's got the film all ready."

Spergyle said, "Keneally isn't coming. I made that up to get Bucky off my back."

JULIA SCHWERDLOFF BUSH

It was going to be just awful but we had to tell Bucky the truth: there was no movie and no Ferris. He would have to call off the premiere. We decided I should tell him as soon as he got to the airport.

But Bucky never came. His driver Joquim came. Bucky had called a press conference at the house to show reporters the shelf he had cleared for the Academy Awards the movie was going to win. He can be so cute, it's sad.

By the time we got to the house, Bucky had left for the theater. When we got to the theater, it was already eight o'clock. Bucky was in the lobby waiting for us. He said, "Come on! It's about to start!"

Meelie turned to me. I didn't know how I could ever tell him this. I said, "Wait, Bucky. We have something to tell you. But before we tell you, we want you to know that we love you very much, and that no matter how smart and successful a person is, he can't always succeed one hundred percent of the time." I was about to say, "There is no movie," when I heard, "These must be the glamorous Schwerdloff sisters I've heard so much about."

I turned to see who was speaking. It was Ferris Keneally. He said, "I've just come from the projection booth and the film's all ready." Standing next to him was his daughter, a beautiful girl.

Bucky said, "Well, great! Let's go get our seats!"

Ferris escorted his daughter in, then Meelie and I went in with Bucky. Bucky was wearing Daddy's tuxedo and he looked very handsome.

CHAPTER 12

THE PREMIERE

CANDY LA FORCE, *Eye On News,* KJCK, Los Angeles, June 30, 1985

"My Progress" says you, Ferris Keneally! If this is Progress, I don't want it! P.U.! No thanks! Get lost! This is your Arts and Culture editor . . .

PRESIDENT REAGAN, news conference, July 10, 1985

. . . Yes, I do, uh, think there will be some movement very favorable to our side at the arms talks this fall. I think you could . . . well, I predict that Mr. Gorbachev will be very eager to sign an agreement with us. That's because they know they can never come up with as big a bomb as *The Pilgrim's Progress.* (laughs)

PAULINE KAEL, *The New Yorker,* July 15, 1985

. . . You are mesmerized by it though, the same way you can't take your eyes away from a bad car accident. . . .

AMELIA SCHWERDLOFF DUFFEE

I always wanted to be in the military and I knew that someday I might be captured and tortured. So when I was a kid, I trained myself to withstand pain. By the time I was ten, I was able to cook a marshmallow over the fire without a stick. I just held it there. Eventually, I got so I could bake a potato. I could take anything.

Then I sat through Buck's movie and finally, all that training paid off.

The movie. Oh, dear. Well, I'm being too hard. At least no one walked out. Of course, there was the jeering and the throwing things. In that long, long scene of water going down the drain—that's all the scene was, I still can't believe it, just three minutes of water going down the drain—Chevy Chase ran up to the screen and flashed a moon at it.

Finally, when Katharine Hepburn, who was sitting to Ferris's left, threw her purse at the screen, Ferris stood up and yelled, "Stop the film!"

Everyone saw that it was Ferris and became very quiet. He walked up to the front of the theater. Katharine Hepburn told me later she thought he was going to get her purse back. But then he said, "This is not my film!" He pointed to Bucky. "You've butchered it!"

I turned to tell Bucky I really liked the movie but he had fainted.

DR. YALE ZIMET

I was pleased by Ferris's behavior. While it was cruelly inaccurate and immoral of him to blame Bucky, on the positive side, it was good that he knew someone had to be blamed. The first step in blaming ourselves is to blame others.

I took Bucky home. I didn't want him to be alone. When we got home, Bucky changed into his pajamas and we turned on the TV. Bucky wanted to see the reviews.

They were, well, you know, the worst reviews ever written about any film ever made. First that screening, now this. I didn't know how much more Bucky could take. But then he just flipped off the TV and said, "Well, those are only the TV critics. This film is too intellectual for them. What really matters are the newspaper reviews."

He was sitting on the edge of his bed, trying to get his slipper off. He said, "The thing I don't understand is Ferris. Why did he say that about me? I thought he liked me." He gave up trying to get the slipper off and just got into bed. He said, "I guess he's a very sick man."

I said good night and he said, "Julia? Thanks for coming out. It meant a lot to have you here tonight."

SARAH PAYNE, ad director at the Mr. Schwerdloff Studio

We tried a lot of different campaigns for *My Progress.* I think our most daring ad was the one where we took out a two-page spread, quoting *Newsweek's* review, "TERRIBLE AND HORRIFIC!" We'd hoped people would misread that as "TERRIFIC!"

We were all demoralized, except Mr. Schwerdloff. I ran into him in the middle of this, and he said, "Reviews never mean a thing. It's the public who decides."

Meelie left the next day but I decided to wait around to be with Bucky when "the verdict," as he called it, came in. That would be Monday when the figures were reported from the theaters about how many people saw the film over the weekend.

I dreaded Monday. Bucky was going to be devastated and I didn't know what I could do to protect him.

As soon as he got up Monday he called the studio. Someone gave him the figures and they were worse than we ever feared. Oh, dear. Over the whole weekend in over thirty theaters throughout all of Los Angeles only two people came to the movie. As if that weren't bad enough, apparently one of the people didn't even pay. This poor man was flying over the Loew's Acropolis when his plane ran out of gas and he crashed into the theater.

Bucky tried not to be discouraged. He said, "There must be a reason for this." So he called up the research people and asked them to find out if the reason that only two people came to the movie was that there had been so many people at the premiere. The research people attributed the low turnout to the poor reviews.

After he hung up with the research people, Bucky said to me, "Well, we're not dead yet! Everyone knows that bad reviews don't mean a thing if you've got good word of mouth."

So, I mean, I feel silly telling it now, but we drove to a lot of malls, and walked up to people and told them how great *My Progress* was. One little boy we saw was crying because he'd lost his dog. Bucky told him it was inside the UA Coronet where *My Progress* was showing.

We got back, and it was so sad, Bucky was just desperate. He started making random phone calls. If a man answered, he'd tell him he didn't want to identify himself but that he'd just seen the man's wife going into the next show of *My Progress* with another man, and if the man hurried and bought a ticket, the man could still catch them.

Bucky was all alone. No one was helping him. That awful Ferris—I shouldn't say that, I know he's mentally unbalanced, but still—that awful Ferris gave a lot of interviews denouncing the film, saying he had wanted to do a big sci-fi movie but Bucky had forced him to make *My Progress* on a legal technicality.

The final blow was the headline of that week's *Variety*: "MY PROGRESS: NUMBER ONE FLOP OF ALL TIME; SCHWERDLOFF JR. FAILS BIG; LETS SIBS AND DEAD FATHER DOWN."

There it was. He couldn't avoid it any longer.

When Bucky saw the headline, he folded the paper and calmly placed it on the table—too calmly, it was eerie. He walked to the window and looked out. I was just terrified. I thought, *He's going to crack.* When he turned back to me, there was a jagged line across his face and it ran from his ear to his chin. *My God,* I thought, *he is cracking!* But it was a shadow from the blinds.

When he spoke his voice was very hoarse—he said, "I can't—I've never felt—I've got to have air."

He walked outside. I watched through the window. He went to the sidewalk and stared at some dirt. Then, after a long time, he bent over. It was too pathetic. I couldn't look anymore.

Until *My Progress* I had never failed at anything. In lots of ways, this was good, but what happened was each time I didn't fail, I'd be more nervous that the next time, I would fail—because, I mean, I had to fail sometime, it just wasn't human. And then *My Progress* happened and I failed, I really failed. I tried not to admit it for a while, but then the *Variety* came out and I had to face it.

I was too embarrassed to be in the room with Julia. It was partly for her sake that I'd done the whole thing. I could tell she felt sad for me and I didn't want that. If anyone was going to feel sorry for me, it would be me. That may make me old-fashioned, but that's the kind of man I am: I do things for myself.

I went outside and walked down the street. I wanted to walk forever. Then I saw a red bike propped against a tree. It was just like the bike I'd had when I was a kid, only it didn't have the little silver bell. I hadn't ridden a bike since I was a kid but I remembered how nice it was to ride and to feel the wind on my face. When I rode my bike, I felt like I could run the world.

I decided to ride it. As soon as I picked it up, I felt better. I got on and pushed off. I'd only ridden about a foot when I fell over. It was weird. It was like I'd never ridden before. I couldn't keep my balance. I tried again, but this time I only got half a foot. I couldn't get anywhere. I wanted to cry. I used to ride my bike every day. Why was this happening to me? I'll tell you, I was very scared. Then I thought: the movie, now this. I can't be defeated twice. It will set a pattern.

This time, I got on and I vowed to make it. I got two and a half feet. I would have gotten farther, only I was pointed at the curb and I couldn't steer away from it. I tore my shirt when I fell, but it didn't matter. This wasn't about shirts. This was about something bigger. I analyzed what I was doing wrong. I thought really hard what to do, then I pushed off.

I rode down the block. Pretty soon, I got good. I could ride without my hands and, when I rode under a tree, I pulled the leaves off a twig and threw them behind me. I got so confident, I closed my eyes and rode through a busy intersection.

There was a big hill and I pedaled to the top. The wind was blowing and it felt good. I was breathing hard. Failure was out of my system.

EPILOGUE

THE QUESTION MOST ASKED IN THOSE DAYS WAS, "CAN ONE MOVIE REALLY BREAK A STUDIO?" AS ONE WALKS ACROSS THE GROUNDS OF WHAT WAS ONCE HOLLYWOOD'S MOST PRESTIGIOUS AND SUC-CESSFUL LOT AND IS NOW THE LARGEST PEPSI COLA BOTTLING PLANT WEST OF THE MISSISSIPPI, ONE HAS ONE'S ANSWER.

THE STUDIO WAS SOLD IN EARLY 1985 AFTER THE FAMOUS SCHWERDLOFF AUCTION WHERE DEBBIE REYNOLDS PAID $120,000 FOR THE GOLF SHOES THAT JEAN ARTHUR WORE TO HER HURRIED WEDDING WITH JAMES STEWART IN *LET'S PLAY GOLF*. THIS WAS THE HIGHEST PRICE EVER PAID FOR SHOES IN AN AUCTION. A MORE SENTIMENTAL SALE WAS MADE TO BUCKY SCHWERDLOFF. SCHWERD-LOFF PURCHASED THE TWO SHAWLS FROM *THE TWO SHAWLS OF CARLOTTA* FOR HIS SISTERS.

THE YEAR 1985 WAS NOTABLE FOR ANOTHER REASON. FRIAR CURRIE, BACK IN THE MONASTERY, RECEIVED THE WELCOME NEWS THAT HIS FILM WAS TO BE SHOWN BY THE ORSON WELLES THEATER (CAMBRIDGE, MASSACHUSETTS). HE HAD SENT IT THERE ON THE AD-VICE OF ONE OF THE HERMITS. THE FILM WAS SHOWN THE SAME WEEK THAT A GROUP OF LEADING FILM CRITICS MET IN CAMBRIDGE TO HONOR BERTHOLD LEITHAUSER. LEITHAUSER, WHO WAS SUP-POSED TO BE AT A SHERRY WITH HARVARD'S PRESIDENT DEREK BOK, CAUGHT A MATINEE OF CURRIE'S FILM. THAT NIGHT, AT HIS HONOR-ARY DINNER, LEITHAUSER TOLD THE AUDIENCE THAT THE FILM WAS ONE OF THE TRUE ORIGINALS OF THE SCREEN. THE CRITICS FLOCKED

TO SEE *THE PILGRIM'S PROGRESS* AND GAVE IT WIDE PRAISE: ". . . A FILM SO COURAGEOUS IT HAS NO ACTION, NO DRAMA—BARELY EVEN ANY MOVEMENT. IT RIVETS . . ." (ANDREW SARRIS, *THE VILLAGE VOICE*); "IT IS A LITTLE FILM. A SMASHING AND WITTY LITTLE FILM. ITS AMBITION IS TO HAVE NO AMBITION. NOT ONLY DOES IT NOT HAVE DOLBY SOUND AND EXPENSIVE SPECIAL EFFECTS, IT IS RIPPED IN SOME PLACES." (VINCENT CANBY, *THE NEW YORK TIMES*).

IKE SPERGYLE WAS NOT SO LUCKY. HE WENT TO COLUMBIA PICTURES, WHERE, AT FIRST, HE HAD A SUCCESSFUL SLATE OF FILMS. THEN, COLUMBIA BOUGHT WINDMILL PICTURES, AN INDEPENDENT PRODUCTION COMPANY WHICH WAS PRODUCING FERRIS KENEALLY'S NEW MOVIE. THE THOUGHT OF WORKING WITH KENEALLY AGAIN SO UNNERVED SPERGYLE THAT HE URGED HIS SUPERIORS AT COLUMBIA TO CANCEL KENEALLY'S PROJECT. WHEN THEY REFUSED, SPERGYLE LEFT COLUMBIA FOR UNIVERSAL. KENEALLY'S FILM, PRODUCED THAT YEAR BY COLUMBIA, WAS THE TOP-GROSSING FILM OF THE YEAR.

AS KENEALLY TOLD US, "BEFORE *MY PROGRESS*, I MADE FILMS FOR THE MASSES. I DID *MY PROGRESS* TO LEARN TO LOVE MORE MYSELF AND I LEARNED SOMETHING VERY IMPORTANT: I PREFER MASS ADORATION TO MY OWN." KENEALLY IS NO LONGER BITTER ABOUT *MY PROGRESS* AND SAYS HE REGRETS BLAMING SCHWERDLOFF. "THAT WAS NOT CRICKET OF ME," HE TOLD US, "NOT HONORABLE, AND LOOK, LOOK HERE, I DON'T WANT TO SING SONGS ABOUT MYSELF BUT I AM, ABOVE ALL ELSE, A MAN OF HONOR."

THE FILM THAT RESTORED KENEALLY TO HIS LOFTY POSITION AS KING OF THE BOX OFFICE WAS, *YOUNGER THAN YESTERDAY*, ABOUT A MOTHER AND FATHER WHO, THROUGH A FREAK ACCIDENT WITH A MICROWAVE, BECOME ONE YEAR YOUNGER EVERY DAY.

WHEN BUCKY SCHWERDLOFF LEARNED THAT KENEALLY HAD MADE A MOVIE OF HIS IDEA, HE WAS GENEROUS. HE SAID, "I'M HAPPY FOR FERRIS THAT HE IS FINALLY SECURE ENOUGH TO TAKE HELP, TO LOOK TO OTHERS."

AS FOR SCHWERDLOFF, HE IS BUSY PLANNING A NEW PROJECT: HE IS HOPING TO BUILD A CHAIN OF PRIVATE POST OFFICES ACROSS THE NATION TO COMPETE WITH THE UNITED STATES POST OFFICE.

"YOU KNOW," HE SAYS, "A STAMP IS A PIECE OF PAPER SMALLER THAN MY THUMB BUT EACH ONE COSTS TWENTY-TWO CENTS. SOMEBODY IS DOING SOMETHING *WRONG*. I KNOW I CAN MAKE A STAMP CHEAPER THAN THAT." SCHWERDLOFF TOLD US THAT HIS FIRST STAMP WOULD BE OF HIS FATHER SITTING AT HIS DESK ANSWERING HIS PHONE.

THE SCHWERDLOFF SISTERS VEHEMENTLY OPPOSE THEIR BROTHER'S NEW BUSINESS IDEA. THEY TRIED EVERYTHING THEY COULD TO DISSUADE HIM BUT TO NO AVAIL. FINALLY, THEY TOLD HIM HOW THEY HAD CONTRIVED AND SUPPORTED EVERY SUCCESS HE HAD EVER HAD. "AREN'T THEY CUTE?" BUCKY ASKED US. "THEY'RE MY SISTERS BUT THEY ACT LIKE MY MOTHER. THEY WERE AFRAID I'D HAVE ANOTHER EXPERIENCE LIKE *MY PROGRESS*. THAT'S WHY THEY MADE UP ALL THAT STUFF ABOUT THE BUSINESSES. THEY WERE TRYING TO PROTECT ME.

"THEY WERE VERY UPSET ABOUT *YOUNGER THAN YESTERDAY*, MY *COUNTDOWN* IDEA. MEELIE WANTED TO SUE FERRIS, BUT I JUST DON'T THINK YOU SUE SOMEONE WHO'S BEEN IN A MENTAL HOME. BESIDES, IT'S NOT THE LAST GREAT IDEA I'M GOING TO HAVE. I'M ALWAYS GETTING IDEAS."

A WORD FROM THE AUTHORS

THERE HAS BEEN SOME CONTROVERSY IN THE PRESS ABOUT *BLOCK-BUSTER*, STEMMING FROM THE NUMEROUS PREPUBLICATION LAW-SUITS AGAINST US. THE MEDIA, WITH ITS FLAIR FOR THE SENSATIONAL, CONSISTENTLY MISREPRESENTED THE FACTS. TO SET THE RECORD STRAIGHT, WE OFFER SUMMARIES AND OUTCOMES OF THE CASES, QUOTED FROM THE COURT LOGS.

Spergyle vs. Marx and McGrath: Spergyle charges that Marx and McGrath defamed his character by claiming that he engaged in sex acts with Simone Bejour. According to Spergyle, the evidence used by the authors—namely the oral testimony of Simone Bejour and Ferris Keneally—was "a fiction, fabricated by the authors to add sex to their book in a desperate attempt to increase sales." Marx refuted this by producing a photograph of Spergyle and Bejour in a bathtub, which Marx had found in Spergyle's suitcase on a love weekend she shared with Spergyle in Paris. Spergyle maintained that the picture was "doctored" and told the court, "I have never been to Paris with Ms. Marx. I am a happily married man."

McGrath vs. Marx: "McGrath contends that he is enti-tled to 3/5 of the royalties because, "I just did more than Patty—by far." He further alleges that:

1. Marx conspired to interview Barbra Streisand, McGrath's "very, very favorite singing actress in the world," on the day McGrath had arranged to have his hair transplanted. "She knew I wanted to meet Barbra Streisand more than anything in the whole world," McGrath testified, "but Patty had to hog her."

2. McGrath bore the bulk of utilities costs as all writing was done at McGrath's apartment. McGrath told the court, "The lights I don't care about—I would've left them on for the plants anyway—but the water! She uses water like nobody's business! I'm not going to describe how, but she knows what I mean."

3. "She just doesn't pay attention. When we were writing the history of the Mr. Schwerdloff Studio, I distinctly told her to write down what we said. She said she thought I said that I would write down what we said. When we completed the chapter after three weeks, we learned that nothing had been written down and we had to start all over again."

South Africa vs. McGrath and Marx: "The government of South Africa charges that McGrath and Marx obstructed the passage of their shipping vessels through the Mozambique Channel, resulting in the massive spoilage of Granny Smith apples."

OUTCOMES

May 25, 1987

South Africa vs. McGrath vs. Marx: Suit was dismissed after four months when McGrath and Marx realized South Africa was confusing "McGrath & Marx" with the country of "Madagascar." "No hard feelings," McGrath and Marx said on their way out of court. "We get their mail all the time."

June 1, 1987
McGrath vs. Marx: The jury sided with McGrath. In addition to restructured royalties, Marx was ordered, at McGrath's request, to give McGrath the hair she had taken as a souvenir from Streisand's brush.

September 27, 1987
Spergyle vs. Marx and McGrath: Judge D'Agostino dismissed the suit when she discovered that Ike Spergyle was a fictional character.